NIKKI COPLESTON worked in London for many years before moving back to the West Country where she was brought up. In 2016, she published the award-winning *The Shame of Innocence*, featuring DI Jeff Lincoln, and is currently rewriting an earlier Jeff Lincoln crime novel, *The Price of Silence*.

Nikki is a member of Frome Writers' Collective, which supports and promotes writers in the area round Frome. She's also a founder member of Stellar Scribes, a group of novelists from Wells and Glastonbury who love to share their passion for a good yarn, mainly through talks and events in libraries.

Fascinated by history, she enjoys exploring with her camera, photographing landscapes and quirky architecture, old and new. She and her husband now live in Wells, Somerset, with their cat.

Connect with the author on:
Facebook.com/nikki.coplesto:
Twitter: @nikkicopleston
Website: nikkicopleston.com

C000161743

A SAIN†LY GRAVE DISTURBED

NIKKI COPLESTON

SilverWood

Originally published in 2017 as an ebook by sBooks
an imprint of SilverWood Books Ltd

This paperback edition published by SilverWood Books 2018

SilverWood Books Ltd
14 Small Street, Bristol, BS1 1DE, United Kingdom
www.silverwoodbooks.co.uk

ISBN 978-1-78132-834-7 (paperback)
ISBN 978-1-78132-691-6 (ebook)

British Library Cataloguing in Publication Data
A CIP catalogue record for this book is available from the British Library

Page design and typesetting by SilverWood Books
Printed on responsibly sourced paper

MONDAY

1

The first bones came up at five in the afternoon, as the light was fading and everyone was feeling the cold through the soles of their feet.

'Careful, careful.' Greg held his hands under the tray as Beth and Sandy lifted it clear of the grave.

Beth frowned down at him, irritated, as she and Sandy gently laid the tray of bones on the grass. 'We've done this before, Greg. You're fussing like a new mother.'

'It feels a bit like that,' he said, clambering out of the grave. 'My first proper dig. You two are old hands at this, so the novelty's worn off.'

Sandy shook his head. 'The novelty never wears off, Greg. No two digs are the same. That's why I come back year after year.'

Beth made no comment. As one of the few professionals among them, she valued volunteers like Sandy and Greg, but longed for the day when she wouldn't need them – though that day was unlikely to come, given the pathetic budgets allocated to an excavation like this. Luckily, she and Josh – who was working on a trench the other side of Abbey Green – could afford occasionally to take on a project like this one, even though it paid peanuts.

Sandy McFarlane, wiry and agile, had been a member of the local archaeology group for six or seven years, but Greg Baverstock was a newbie. When Beth had first met him a few days ago, she'd thought he was too big: tall and broad, with a bit of a paunch, not built for squatting in trenches for hours on end scraping away at ancient burials. Yet he'd moved with surprising ease for a man in his late forties, built like a rugby prop who's gone to seed.

'He looks awful small for a monk,' Sandy said, studying the tibia of the skeleton they'd unearthed, although he wasn't allowed to handle it yet. 'Awful short in the leg.'

Beth had to agree but reminded him that monasteries took in people with deformities or injuries, who couldn't make their way in the outside world. 'This guy could've been too weak to put out in the fields or into a workshop. Maybe he was a young orphan the abbot took in to serve in the kitchens.'

'A medieval kitchen boy!' Sandy peeled off his gloves so he could help her with the tray. 'How about that!'

'Are we sure these bones are medieval?' Greg asked, peering back down into the trench.

'Of course they are. The abbey's been here since the eighth century.' Beth bit her lip in concentration as she eased the bones into a plastic sleeve that would protect them until she could get them back to the museum, on the other side of Abbey Green. 'Why d'you ask?'

'I was wondering about the watch,' said Greg, jumping down into the trench and retrieving something from the rubble. He held aloft a tarnished wristwatch, too small to belong to anyone but a child. Fragments of the strap were still attached. 'Not that I'm an expert, but it doesn't look very medieval, does it?'

2

On the other side of Barbury, Detective Inspector Jeff Lincoln unlocked the door of his new home and stepped inside. The Old Vicarage had officially become his a couple of months ago, but he was still excited about it. Until the end of last year, he'd been stuck in a bedsit in a gloomy street near the centre of town, but now he could look forward to moving into a rambling Edwardian house on the outskirts.

Not that his house was ready to move into quite yet. The electrics had been sorted and the gas supply restored. He'd even found a company that replaced sash windows, and through his sergeant, Mike Woods, he'd tracked down a roofer who could start work in a couple of weeks. For now, though, the place was fit only for the occasional visit to check nobody was squatting there or using the floorboards for impromptu barbecues on the back verandah – as had happened a few weeks ago.

His mobile trilled in his jacket pocket. He was off duty and considered ignoring it, but knew it could be something important. He recognised the number. 'Woody?'

'Serious assault on the Barbury Down estate, boss. Sounds like a straightforward domestic, but I reckon you'll want to deal with it.'

Something in Woody's voice unsettled him. 'What aren't you telling me?'

'Gracie Bell's involved.'

Lincoln's cheerful mood evaporated. Gracie was one of those young women who got involved with the wrong man, escaping only to get involved with another one who treated her every bit as badly. He hadn't seen her since her ex-husband was sent down last year for trying to set her flat on fire with her in it. He dreaded to think what had happened to her now. 'How serious?'

'The bloke's in hospital and Gracie's been arrested. She's being brought in now.'

Lincoln sighed, relieved at least that it wasn't Gracie who'd ended up in hospital. 'OK. I'll be there as soon as I can.' He locked the Old Vicarage up again and drove back to Barley Lane police station.

One of the two fluorescent tubes in the interview room was on the blink and kept flickering. Across the table, shoulders hunched, sat Gracie Bell: twenty-nine, a bit overweight, face flushed, henna-streaked hair tangled and dry. Her right wrist was bound in a snowy-white bandage.

Lincoln went through the formalities with her, introducing himself and DC Pam Smyth.

'I remember you from before, Mr Lincoln.' Gracie blinked slowly as if she was drugged or drunk. Her gaze slid over Lincoln's face and settled on Pam's. 'Is Ade gonna be OK?'

'Mr Gomez is in a stable condition,' Pam said. 'You stabbed him four or five times.'

'Five.' Gracie fidgeted with her bandage. 'Once for every bitch he's fucked since we've been together.'

Lincoln had some photos in front of him: the scene of the attack in a sparsely furnished council flat on the edge of Barbury Down. Blood had pooled on the laminate floor. A dining chair was on its side next to an upturned coffee table and pottery ornaments lay smashed in the empty hearth. Beer cans and wine bottles were lined up on the windowsill, and clothes and a duvet were heaped on the sofa. 'You admit to stabbing him? Tell us what happened.'

When Gracie got home from work at five o'clock, she said, her key wouldn't turn in the lock. Adrian worked nights so she knew he'd be there. Guessed he'd put the deadbolt on so she couldn't walk in on him and his latest girlfriend.

When she opened the letterbox and heard them moaning, she smashed the window in the door, reached in and unhitched the lock. With blood oozing from cuts on her wrist and arm, she'd confronted Adrian – but only after she'd grabbed a kitchen knife from the block on the worktop.

'He's sex-mad, that's what he is. Wouldn't mind if he give *me* some every now and again, but he hasn't been interested in fucking *me* for weeks.'

'Do you know the girl he was with?' Lincoln asked. She'd fled by the time the police arrived on the scene, and Gomez had been too weak to tell them anything.

'Mia. Kia. Tia. Something the fuck like that. Bitch fucking threw up over my clean floor.'

He could see as much in the photographs – the vomit, not the clean floor. Gracie's standards of hygiene were not the same as most people's.

Pam shook her head, puzzled. 'Why didn't you chuck him out the first time he was unfaithful?'

'Because, for all his faults, I love him.' Gracie started to cry. 'And now I'm scared I've killed him.'

3

Next morning, Lincoln found himself standing in the grounds of Barbury Abbey, slowly sinking into soft mud. He'd have put gumboots on if he'd realized the soggy state of the ground.

Apart from a chainsaw screaming in one of the gardens that bordered Abbey Green, this part of Barbury was a quiet sanctuary. The air was chilly even for spring, though, and all he could think of was getting some hot coffee inside him.

In front of him, a young woman stood in what looked like a shallow swimming pool that had been drained a thousand years ago. Flags and tape, surveying poles and metal markers outlined the extent of the excavation that had been underway for the past few days. Fifty yards away, a trench the size of a kiddies' paddling pool seemed to be full of people kneeling or squatting with trowels or shovels.

He could think of better ways to spend the Easter holidays.

'So, where are the remains now?' he asked the young woman who'd reported the find a couple of hours earlier.

'We took it to the museum yesterday evening.' Tarrant, she'd said her name was, Beth Tarrant – an archaeological consultant, whatever that was. Her light brown hair was tightly plaited in beaded cornrows, and in her rainbow striped jumper and denim jeans, she looked more like a student from Barbury Community College than a professional historian.

'You should have left the skeleton in situ, Miss Tarrant.'

'When we brought the bones out of the grave, we assumed a death date of somewhere in the tenth or eleventh century. It was only when one of the volunteers spotted a wristwatch…'

'Yes, that *would* give you pause for thought.'

She sighed dramatically. 'The bones are old but they're not old *enough*. No point contacting the authorities last night, so we took them across to the museum, where someone could examine them in more detail today. They've got the facilities there.'

'So have we,' said Lincoln. 'The hospital mortuary.' He stepped back before his feet, in lace-up shoes, sank completely into the mud.

Across Abbey Green, the chainsaw was silent while a lopped and rotten tree branch went crashing down into its garden.

He waited while she scrambled up onto the grass. 'Let's go to the museum then.'

Barbury Museum occupied a medieval manor house and was a repository for all things ancient – and not so ancient. Beth led Lincoln along panelled corridors, past display cases and through exhibition spaces until she opened a door onto a windowless room, shelved on all sides like a library for cardboard boxes.

The bones lay in a large metal tray on a table that seemed to fill the room. Dirt still clung to them, though it was starting to dry out and crumble.

'This is pretty much how he was lying in the grave,' Beth said. 'We'd normally be photographing and cleaning him up by now, but I decided to wait and notify the police. The colour of the bones is wrong, you see, and they didn't feel right.'

'You're sure it's a "he"?'

'The pelvis is too narrow to be female.'

Lincoln nodded, though he knew that, until puberty, the shape of the pelvis is an unreliable indicator of gender. Still, Beth Tarrant had no doubt examined more skeletal remains than he had. 'Were you expecting to find human remains there at all?'

She nodded. 'We were hoping to find the grave of Abbot William Spere, the so-called Angling Abbot. He liked to fish.'

'I've never understood the attraction.'

'Me neither.' She gave him a quick smile – kindred spirits. 'There was a chapel there at that time, attached to the west end of the abbey, with a crypt underneath it, and that's where he wanted to be buried, closest to the river bank. Of course, the ground here was really too boggy and the chapel's foundations began to sink. It was pulled down – or fell down – but the crypt with all its tombs was left untouched. When we uncovered this grave yesterday, so close to the river bank, I thought we'd hit the jackpot and found Abbot William.'

She gave Lincoln a rueful smile as she leaned across the table to pick up a small polythene pouch. 'Then one of the volunteers spotted this watch.'

Lincoln peered at it through the plastic. The strap had rotted and was little more than a leather thong with half the metal clasp attached. He could just make out "Timex" on the flaking dial. A child's watch. The back of his neck prickled. 'And where was this?'

'Under the bones. That's what made me suspicious.'

'Could these be the remains of a child?'

Beth shook her head, the beads on her plaits clattering. 'The teeth suggest an adult, probably early twenties. I'd say he's a young man, shorter than average, with healthy teeth – except for a couple of amalgam fillings. That naturally made me query this guy's age, although dentists were using metal to fill teeth as long ago as the 1800s.'

Lincoln laid the wristwatch gently down on the table. 'But not as long ago as the tenth or eleventh century.'

Beth looked sheepish. 'No.'

'You know anyone who can help us out?'

'Actually, I do.'

It didn't take long for an osteo-archaeologist Beth knew to establish that the skeleton was probably no more than a hundred years old. By mid-afternoon, Lincoln could gather his team together in Barley Lane's CID room to give them an update.

'Our abbey skeleton is probably a medical specimen,' he said. 'Now it's been cleaned up, they've found drill holes where the bones were wired together at some stage. The skeleton was probably hung up on a stand and used as a teaching aid for medical students. You must've seen the sort of thing I mean in old films.'

Breeze began to sing under his breath. *'The thigh bone's connected to the...shin bone, and the shin bone's connected to the –'* A frown from Lincoln silenced him.

'He looks all out of proportion,' said Pam. 'Top-heavy.'

'Must've been a bit of a short-arse,' Breeze agreed with a laugh. 'Finding trousers to fit must've been tricky, especially with no internet.'

'Either way,' said Lincoln, trying to restore order, 'the bones aren't recent and they aren't medieval. Our skeleton was probably nicked from the local hospital and – what's the word? Disarticulated?'

'But what was it doing buried where an old monk was supposed to be?' Breeze laid his Subway roll down on a paper towel and licked his fingers. 'I bet the osteo-arky whatsit couldn't tell us *that*!'

'Unfortunately not.' Lincoln perched himself on the edge of the desk. 'That site was last excavated in 1956 by a Professor Lever.' He glanced at the notes of his meeting with Beth. 'And a Doctor Roper-Reid. Beth Tarrant suspects someone on that dig tried to sabotage it with this juvenile prank – burying a skeleton they'd stolen from somewhere and derailing the whole project. Most of the volunteers in 1956 were undergraduates. They'd have thought it was a real hoot to see these esteemed archaeologists scratching their heads over an unexpected grave, I bet. And then the experts would see the kid's watch and know they'd been had. Except it doesn't look as if the 1956 dig ever reached that part of the site, so the skeleton and the watch have been down there ever since.'

'Reckon those students went to a lot of trouble for nothing,' said Woody.

'That's students for you.' Breeze screwed up his paper towel and batted it round the desk. 'A lot of pointless effort just for a laugh.'

'The alignment would've been significant,' Pam put in, studying the dig-site diagram on the board. 'That grave's north-south. A Christian burial would be east-west. If Lever and Roper-Reid had found it, they'd have thought they'd discovered a pre-Christian burial site. They'd have been over the moon.'

Lincoln snorted. 'And they'd have looked pretty foolish when they realized someone had played a trick on them. They'd never have lived it down.'

Beth had been adamant that Lever's notes made no mention of such a discovery, even one that proved mistaken. The students' elaborate joke must have ended as a damp squib.

Breeze folded his beefy arms. 'So, have we even got an investigation now?' he asked, scowling at the whiteboard. 'Some woman digs up a joke skeleton from sixty years ago, and it turns out to be a twentieth-century teaching aid? Hardly a police matter now, is it? I mean, nobody *died*.'

4

Lincoln hated hospitals: the smells, the beeping, the tannoy announcements, the brightly coloured lines on the floor, the blaring large-print signage. Hospitals always made him feel like a child again, and not in a good way.

'Collingwood Ward,' Pam said, pointing. 'That's where they said he is.'

Adrian Gomez's bed was next to a window overlooking a concrete bunker that sounded as if it housed a generator. Before he left Barley Lane, Lincoln had checked the injured man's criminal record. He'd been caught shoplifting as a juvenile and put on probation. He'd also been charged with theft when he was twenty-two, but the charges had been dropped. Since then, he'd apparently led a blameless life.

At forty-four, Gomez was fifteen years older than Gracie Bell, but looked older still, now he was lying propped up on pillows, his face drawn, his arms and chest bandaged. 'She tried to kill me,' he said before Pam had even got her notebook out.

Lincoln borrowed a chair from the other side of the room and sat down. 'Take us through it, as much as you remember.'

Gomez scowled at him, then pressed his head back into the

pillow. 'That bitch came home from work early. Soon as she was through that door, she went for me with a knife, accusing me of having a woman there while she was out.'

'And *had* you had a woman there?' Lincoln needed to know, not because it lessened Gracie's offence, but because Mia or Kia or Tia could be a material witness.

'Of course I fucking had! You think that silly bitch is interested in anything but the money I bring home?'

'Where do you work?'

'Security firm. Abercrombie & Hale. Night shifts mostly. Suits my lifestyle.' He glared down at his bandages. 'Fucking losing money every hour I'm in here. That fucking bitch!'

'We'll need to take a statement,' said Pam, impatiently running a hand through her short blonde hair. 'Are you up to doing that?'

He lifted his hands. 'My signature's gonna be a bit buggered, but I'll sign anything you want if it gets that bitch put somewhere out the way!'

Lincoln stood up and began to walk away. Gracie shouldn't be excused for attacking her lover with a knife, but she'd probably been provoked. 'I suggest you move out of her flat as soon as you can, Mr Gomez. Move out of Barbury, maybe. See if Abercrombie & Hale can find you a nice little job the other side of Presford.'

Gomez made a face. 'I'm happy working where I am, thank you very much. Why should *I* be the one to move away?'

5

'Bloody tedious, having to go back to cleaning sherds.' Greg dumped his glass down on the bar. Work on Beth Tarrant's part of the site had been temporarily suspended, so he and Sandy had been helping Josh Good's team instead. They'd spent most of the day scrubbing washing-up bowls full of pottery fragments found in other parts of the abbey dig site. Nothing as exciting as bones.

'Now they know our skeleton wasn't the victim of foul play, we'll be back digging with Beth again tomorrow, you'll see.' Sandy pulled his wallet out of his jeans pocket, tugged a tenner out. 'Another one?'

Greg wiped his mouth with the back of his hand and checked his watch. 'Not for me, thanks. Couple of phone calls to make.'

'Got to check the wee woman's fine and dandy back home?' Sandy grinned as he flagged down the barman and ordered himself another scotch. 'Sure you won't join me?'

'No, really, thanks.' Greg pushed himself away from the bar and gave Sandy's shoulder a slap. 'See you in the morning. Don't forget your pinny and your Marigolds!'

He pushed his way out of the fug of The Crown. The evening was cool, the streets of Barbury deserted away from the Market

Place, with its bars and restaurants. He didn't know the town well, but when he'd got the chance to work on this dig during the Easter holidays, he'd seized the opportunity: any excuse to get away from Rachel for a bit and indulge his lifelong passion for archaeology.

Along with most of the other volunteers, Greg was staying in student accommodation next to the museum. The rooms were fairly spartan, but a huge improvement on the halls of residence he'd stayed in when he'd been at university aeons ago. His room was on a corner, one window looking out over Abbey Green, the other onto a cobbled courtyard and the river bank beyond. He relished the idea of living simply for a couple of weeks – no luxuries, the bare necessities. Rachel didn't think a room was furnished unless it had a pile of rugs on the floor, loads of cushions on every chair and furry throws on the bed and sofa.

He pulled open the entrance door of the accommodation block and climbed the stairs to his landing two at a time. The communal lights were on timers. One push and they'd stay on long enough, in theory, for you to reach your room before you were plunged into darkness. A bit the worse for wear, he blundered along the upper landing until he reached his door. He patted his pockets for the key, worried for a moment that he'd dropped it in the pub when he pulled his wallet out to buy the first round of drinks, but no – he'd been looking in the wrong pocket.

Then the lights went out. 'Damn!' The key skittered about a bit before it slid into the lock. He turned it, began to push the door open and –

That was the last thing he remembered.

6

Beth Tarrant had always loved old houses – to look at but not to live in. Josh had invited her to stay at his house during the dig, but she wasn't sure his wife would be as keen, especially since they'd only just got back together after separating for a few months. For the next couple of weeks, Beth would be seeing more of Josh than his wife would, so sleeping in their spare room might be a step too far.

Instead, she'd gone on the internet and found an apartment about five minutes' walk from the abbey, in an eighteenth-century house. The flat had low ceilings and its floors sloped haphazardly like the decks of a galleon. Her bathroom was down two short flights of stairs and round a corner, and the fridge was on the landing. Power points were plentiful but in strange places, mostly behind heavy furniture. Still, it wasn't expensive and it had tons of character.

She dumped her soy milk back in the fridge and returned to the tiny kitchen. They had a cheek even calling it a kitchen! Sink and hotplate, microwave above, toaster below, a draining board not much bigger than a sheet of A4.

She yearned to be home in her modern London flat with

the drone of traffic outside her window. Barbury's quiet kept her awake. By the time the dawn chorus started up each morning, she was only just beginning to drift off.

She took her coffee back into the living room and curled up on the window seat overlooking the approach to the abbey. Was this the end of her dig? Could they make up enough time after the red herring of that bloody skeleton? At times like this, she wished she'd been staying at Josh's so they could talk it through, reassure each other that the whole schedule wasn't fucked by one stupid sidetrack.

She'd been drawn to this dig by history. *Family* history. Professor Alfred Lever was her mother's father – a man she'd never met. From the few photos of him that had survived her mother's various house moves and departures, Beth knew he'd been tall and angular, with a long face. A serious moustache made him look old even when he was in his fifties and, despite a severe short-back-and-sides, a wavy lock of dark hair always defied the smoothing effects of Brylcreem.

Barbury Abbey, 1956, was the dig that broke him – or so her mother always said.

'Something happened, Beth,' she'd told her the last time they'd talked about Grandpa Alf. 'He was never the same after he came back.'

'Oh, Mum! How could you remember that? You were only a child yourself!'

'Some things you never forget. I must run.' She'd grabbed the rucksack and rain hat that made her look like a tourist.

'Catch up when you're back, yes? Off anywhere interesting?'

Beth didn't tell her she'd be spending the Easter holidays in Barbury. Not wanting to be quizzed, she'd been vague. 'A bit of a follow-up on our Wessex project, that's all.'

Her mother had given her a quick hug. 'Oh, Lillibet, I do envy you.' Then she was gone.

Beth wished she'd asked her mother what else she knew about the Barbury dig of 1956. What exactly had broken Grandpa Alf? Finding a skeleton that wasn't really old? His notes didn't mention it, but perhaps he'd destroyed them when he realized the grave he and Paul Roper-Reid had discovered was a stupid hoax.

Now she could only hope for enough good weather to continue the dig along the other axis of the trench. She was damned if she was going to ask Josh to help her out, though with any luck, he'd have more than enough finds to keep him occupied in his own part of the site.

Her laptop pinged: a Skype call was coming through from the States. She sat on the floor, her back against the cold radiator, and smiled into the laptop's lens. Troy Benedict's handsome face filled the screen, her own face superimposed in the top corner, nose and cheeks red from wind burn.

'How's the dig coming along?' he was eager to know. 'Found any bodies yet?' He grinned.

She grinned back, deciding to tell him at least a little about the past couple of days. As a fellow archaeologist, he'd understand the frustration of a dig derailed by a misleading find, but she didn't want him to feel sorry for her or think she wasn't up to the job.

She'd looked up to him ever since their first meeting at Exeter University. She'd been an undergraduate, while Troy – several years into his first professional posting, but still lauded by her lecturers as a star student – had been invited back to talk about His Brilliant Career. Even then, he'd already fronted a television series on the Middle Ages and made regular appearances as a talking head on other people's history programmes.

Since then, he'd worked on high-profile projects in the Hebrides and Central America, and now had tenure at a university in California. Despite his success, though, she suspected he secretly yearned for the days when he'd been more hands-on.

'We found some bones yesterday,' she said, 'but they were left over from a much later burial. The grave looked real enough, probably found when the Victorians dug up the abbey grounds in 1880-something, but that lot were more interested in finding treasure than preserving the archaeology. If they found any remains, they dumped them out any old how and filled the grave in again – leaving us to sort out their muddle afterwards!'

'You sound kinda mad.' His Home Counties accent had a distinctly transatlantic twang these days.

'We wasted time I'd sooner have spent excavating more of the crypt.'

'Shit happens. I wish I could come over there, give you a hand.'

Beth's pulse raced. She'd be thrilled to work with him, but might he want to take over? On the other hand, she and Josh could do with all the help they could get, especially after she'd lost valuable time on a grave that had yielded nothing but humiliation.

'That'd be terrific,' she managed to say, 'but we may have to wrap things up soon if the weather changes for the worse.'

'Just don't wrap it up before I get there!' He grinned again, his eyes sparkling, his perfect white teeth flashing.

Once the screen was blank again, Beth sat and calmed herself. Wouldn't it be great if Troy could come over! How long would it take him to arrange flights, though, and get himself from Heathrow? He'd never get here in time.

Her mobile rang as she was about to get ready for bed. It was Sandy, one of the volunteers.

'Greg's been attacked,' he said, his voice frantic. 'He's got a fractured skull. It was me that found him. I'm at the hospital now. Beth, they need to contact his next of kin. They're not sure he'll pull through.'

WEDNESDAY

7

Lincoln looked round the simply furnished room where Greg Baverstock had been staying while he worked on the abbey dig. The modern red-brick accommodation block behind the museum was used for students during term time, for conference delegates during the summer break and, this Easter vacation, for volunteers working with Beth Tarrant and Josh Good.

The latest news from the hospital had not been encouraging. Baverstock had been attacked after he'd got back from the pub last night and may have been lying on the floor of his room for at least an hour before he was found. That hour's delay could make all the difference to whether or not he pulled through.

No weapon had been found, but he'd suffered a serious blow to the back of his head as well as being punched in the face. Right now, nine or ten hours after the likely time of the attack, his life hung in the balance.

The room had been trashed, Baverstock's books, clothes and laptop thrown on the floor. Even his iPod had been trampled underfoot, its docking station smashed against the wall and left in pieces. Lincoln wondered what sort of music he listened to, guessing it wasn't the old jazz he liked himself.

'So how did his attacker get in?' He turned to Pam, who was checking the wardrobe, where only a khaki jacket and a couple of dark fleeces hung.

'The downstairs door isn't kept locked. Anyone could've got into the building and waited on the landing for him to come back.'

'Were they searching for something, d'you think, or messing it up for the sake of it?'

Pam had already been to the hospital to collect Baverstock's clothes for Forensics. 'His wallet was still in his jacket,' she said, 'and quite a bit of cash, but his phone's missing. It's an iPhone, according to the guy I spoke to at the hospital, the one who found him.'

'McFarlane?'

'Yes, Sandy McFarlane. He said he'd come up here to show Greg a magazine article he'd got, something they'd been talking about in the pub. Saw his light on and assumed he was still up. When he got here, the door was ajar and the poor guy was lying on the floor with his head split open.'

Lincoln glanced round, saw a magazine flung down on the chair inside the door: *Archaeology Now,* open at a page on hoaxes.

'Piltdown Man's the one everybody knows about,' he said. 'Some joker faking proof of the missing link between man and the apes. He had the anthropologists fooled for decades.' He cast the magazine aside. 'Not sure the hoax Beth Tarrant uncovered was of quite the same magnitude.'

'And what's that got to do with the attack? It's not as if Greg's important. As Sandy said at the hospital, the volunteers are there to scrape soil and wash pots.'

'I think they do a bit more than that but, yes, I take your point. A case of mistaken identity? Were they after Beth Tarrant and got the wrong room? Did someone think she'd found something valuable in the grave and kept it to herself?'

Pam shook her head. 'According to Sandy, she's staying in a flat somewhere across Abbey Green.'

Lincoln crouched down to inspect the laptop, wondering if it might still be working. He tapped the mousepad and the screen burst into life, with scenic wallpaper and a password prompt.

And that's as far as he could go: he had no authority to look at Baverstock's computer, not unless he died. All he could do for now was make sure it was turned off and its various components kept together. Just in case.

'I can't see his phone anywhere here,' said Pam. 'He could've had it in his hand when he came in and they snatched it off him.'

Lincoln looked round the room again. 'But why do all this damage? If Baverstock surprised a thief going through his stuff, why didn't they take the laptop or the iPod? Why didn't they go through his pockets for his wallet?'

He stepped over a tumble of books to take a look out of the window. A wing of the museum ran parallel, one of its fire exits opening onto the cobbled courtyard shared by the accommodation block. Lawns stretched away down to the river, where mist hovered like a cloud of midges. 'Nice view. You passed his next-of-kin details on to Woody?'

Pam joined him at the window. Should she be leaning so close that he could smell her shampoo? 'He lives with a Rachel Fielder, but we haven't got a number for her – only their address in Warminster. Woody was about to call the local station when I left, see if they could send an officer round.'

'Let's hope Baverstock recovers enough to tell us what happened.'

As he turned away from the window, Lincoln saw something lying on the floor beneath it, close to the skirting board: a coarse wedge of terracotta with a pie-frill edge, looking a bit like a chunk of flower pot.

He stooped to pick it up. 'Does this look old to you?'

Pam took it from him, turning it over and weighing it in the palm of her hand. 'The museum sells replicas of things like this. You don't think it could be the real thing, do you?'

'When you're on a dig, it can't be hard to hide bits of pottery that take your fancy.'

She handed it back. 'But you wouldn't, would you, if you'd volunteered for something like that? It'd be against your principles.'

Lincoln slid the piece of pottery into an evidence bag. 'It'd be against *my* principles, yes, and it'd probably be against *yours*, but we don't know Greg Baverstock from Adam, do we?'

8

Gravel crunched under their feet as Lincoln and Pam approached the imposing entrance of Barbury Museum. Iron bands and hefty studs made the heavy double doors look fortified against intruders, although probably not since the English Civil War had these doors been battered in earnest, when the family who built the manor house supported the wrong side.

'I'm sorry, but we don't open until lunchtime today,' said the elderly woman who answered their knock. It wasn't a door you'd shove your foot into, so Lincoln was quick to show her his warrant card and explain why he and DC Pam Smyth should be let into the museum when the rest of the world was shut out.

'I had no idea,' she said, when they told her about the attack on Greg Baverstock. 'And he's such a nice man. He's spent quite a bit of time here over the past few days, asking about this and that. So gratifying when people show a genuine interest. I do hope he's all right.' She pushed at her perm with a shaky hand. 'Thank the Lord no one tried to break into the museum! Though if they'd tried, every alarm in the place would've gone off!'

Her name was Marjorie and she confirmed that the outside of the complex was covered by CCTV cameras. Being a mere volunteer, though, she had neither the authority nor the know-how to provide Lincoln with the footage that might show comings and goings from the accommodation block next door.

'Lorna, our curator, is on leave – school holidays,' she put in by way of explanation as she picked up the phone behind the counter, 'so I'll have to give Melvyn a tinkle. He's the Facilities Manager.'

While they waited for Melvyn to arrive, and Marjorie put the kettle on, they took a look round, Lincoln feeling guilty that he hadn't made more time to explore the history of the town and its surroundings.

'Some of these figurines are over twenty thousand years old!' Pam exclaimed, her voice hushed as she peeked into one of the glass cases full of clay pots and ornaments. 'Look at that little Venus figure, the pregnant woman!'

She was pointing at a Hovis-coloured statue no more than three or four inches high – a bulbous shape with tiny feet, a feature-less face, huge breasts – were they breasts? Lincoln wasn't sure – and a massive belly.

'Some sort of fertility doll?' he ventured.

'Probably. Isn't it exquisite, though, and so old!'

Marjorie set a tray of mugs down on the counter. 'I wish they didn't have to go digging up graves,' she remarked. 'I'm not superstitious, but if people have been lain to rest, then that's how they should remain. Those monks in the abbey grounds were buried with full Christian ceremony and they shouldn't be disturbed.'

Lincoln picked up a mug of coffee and spooned plenty of sugar into it. 'You don't approve of the excavations?'

'I know archaeology's supposed to help us understand the past better, but opening graves seems like sacrilege. Any bones they find in that crypt will belong to men and boys who gave their lives to God. They should be left in peace.'

'The archaeologists treat the remains with great respect,' Pam assured her.

But Marjorie didn't look about to be swayed.

'Is there anything here about the earlier excavations of the site?' Lincoln pulled himself away from a display of crockery from the Dark Ages. The landscape round Barbury seemed to be bristling with such artefacts – or had been, before they were dug up and put on show here.

'You'll find the Local Studies library in town has the bulk of written records about both the earlier digs. If you give the librarian a ring, I'm sure she'll be able to help you. Ask for Miss Whittington.'

Lincoln put his mug down at the mention of Trish Whittington. Only a few hours ago, he'd slid out of her bed so he could get ready for work without waking her – although she'd woken up anyway and insisted on making him toast and coffee.

Trish was indeed an excellent librarian, not always such a good judge of people, as he'd learnt to his cost at the end of last year. She'd got in the way when he was trying to pin a murder charge on a man she believed to be innocent – and she'd nearly sabotaged the case.

Now, though, he and Trish were living together while the Old Vicarage was being put to rights. Once it was finished, or at least fit to move into, he'd have no excuse to stay on at her house. Since she'd made it very clear that she and her daughter Kate were perfectly happy where they were, he knew she wouldn't be moving in with him.

'Yes,' he said. 'We know Miss Whittington.'

'I remember when they dug it all up before,' Marjorie went on, lifting her mug with both hands to keep it steady. '1956. I'd just left school and started work at the telephone exchange. I used to walk round the abbey in my lunch hour to get some fresh air. They let you get right up to where they were working. Professor Lever was famous, of course, but it was Paul Roper-Reid who was the star! He was often on the wireless and he had such a *wonderful* voice. Quite the artist, too! Such a shame it all ended the way it did.'

'How do you mean?' Pam asked, but then a short, square man with a thick head of hair and a neat grey beard came storming through the double doors and said he was Melvyn Potts and how could he help?

Marjorie drifted away with the tray of mugs and they didn't see her again.

Melvyn Potts was as co-operative as he had to be, and no more. He seemed unduly reticent, as if he expected to be accused of something besides lax security measures at the accommodation block.

'We fitted keypads to the outer doors,' he said when Lincoln queried the ease with which a non-resident could gain entry, 'but the students kept forgetting the code or passing it on to every Tom, Dick or Harry they happened to meet in the pub. We've never had any trouble since we took the keypads off. People are pretty vigilant, in my experience. I understand,' he added, lowering his voice, 'that Mr Baverstock had been drinking before he was attacked. I'm not saying he was incapable, but obviously if one's intoxicated –'

'He wasn't drunk,' Pam said. 'Not according to Mr McFarlane.'

Potts sniffed, sceptical. 'We'll have to have an urgent review of security as soon as we can. I can assure you I'm taking this very seriously.'

9

Back at Barley Lane, they watched the CCTV footage from the museum.

'We don't even know what we're looking for,' Breeze complained to Lincoln.

'Anything suspicious. Tuesday evening, Baverstock left the pub at about ten-thirty but his attacker could've been lying in wait for some time before that. Sandy McFarlane went up and found him just before midnight, so we need to look for anyone hanging around between about ten and twelve.'

Breeze sighed and returned his gaze to the screen. 'Anyone got hold of his missus yet?'

'Not yet,' said Woody. 'An officer from the local station went round to the house but couldn't get an answer. She could be away.'

'The guy who found him thought Baverstock usually phoned her last thing,' Pam said. 'She probably isn't expecting to hear from him again until tonight. I wonder who she'd phone if she didn't hear from him at the usual time?'

Lincoln checked his emails, checked his phone for an update from the hospital. Thought about who'd get the call if anything happened to him. ICE – In Case of Emergency. Who was listed in his phone or in the front of his diary? Ludicrous that he'd come this far in life without having anyone close enough to be listed in the back of his passport. Christ, did he even have a current passport?

He shivered as if someone, as his mother would've said, had walked over his grave. Without giving himself time to decide against it, he phoned Trish.

She didn't sound as pleased to hear his voice as he was to hear hers.

'Jeff, I'm working. Can't it wait till tonight?'

'I suppose it'll have to.'

'Was it important?'

'Doesn't matter if it is, does it? You're working.'

She sighed down the phone. 'I'm sorry, but I've got someone waiting here with an enquiry. Tell me tonight.'

Stupidly disappointed, he put his phone away and went back to watch the CCTV footage with Breeze. Watching paint dry would have been more entertaining.

Then the museum's fire exit opened.

'Aye-aye,' said Breeze as a figure appeared, carrying a large box. He lowered the box to the ground, keeping his foot in the door to stop it closing. Then, with a movement that was almost balletic, he slid back inside, re-emerging seconds later with another, smaller box. This time he let the door close, picked up both boxes and bore them away across the courtyard, disappearing out of view. The time on the screen was 23:47.

'Buggeration! Sorry, boss, that's not last night, that's Sunday – I scrolled back too far.'

'But could there be a connection? What's this bloke doing taking boxes out of the museum at near-on midnight? Is he up to something? Did Baverstock see something he shouldn't have, something suspicious?'

The man with the boxes was chunky, of average height, the peak of his baseball cap shielding his face from the camera.

'He's not wearing gloves,' Breeze pointed out. 'So, he's not afraid of leaving prints.'

Lincoln picked his phone up. 'I'll get on to Melvyn Potts, the Facilities Manager, see if he knows anything about it.'

But Potts wasn't answering, so all Lincoln could do was leave a voicemail asking him to call him as soon as he got it.

Tuesday night, no one came out of the fire exit with boxes. Instead, they saw a different man, taller and bulkier, arriving on the opposite side of the courtyard and going into the accommodation block. Nearly an hour later, close to eleven, Greg Baverstock returned, pulling open the downstairs door and pressing the light on. Ten minutes later, the door was flung open and the bulky man rushed out, fast disappearing off camera.

'That must be the attacker. He's not carrying a weapon or anything.'

Breeze sped through the next uneventful hour of film until another man arrived and went in.

Lincoln jabbed the screen. 'That must be McFarlane, taking the magazine to show Baverstock. He called 999 at a minute past midnight.'

His desk phone rang. Someone to see him – a Mr Potts.

'I wasn't entirely honest with you earlier,' Melvyn Potts said as soon as Lincoln had shut the door of the interview room. An odour of chips lingered: someone must have brought a takeaway in here rather than eat in the canteen.

Lincoln beckoned to him to sit down. 'Honest about what?'

'We've experienced a series of thefts at the museum. We were hoping to deal with the situation ourselves, but if you've been through the CCTV tapes, you'll have seen what we did: someone's been removing artefacts after hours.'

'And you were going to deal with that yourself?'

Potts folded his hands on the table, displaying immaculately trimmed nails and tidy cuticles with perfect half-moons. 'It was, as you'd say, an inside job.'

'Which is why your alarms didn't go off.'

'Exactly. We took on a new security firm in January instead of employing our own night watchmen. The thefts started not long after, but we couldn't be sure which of their guards was responsible. He knew to hide his face from the cameras. Then we worked out who was working which shift and narrowed it down to one man.'

'You should've come to us as soon as you knew what was going on,' Lincoln said. 'Why use a firm that's employing thieves?'

'We've learnt our lesson there.' He paused, took a deep breath. 'Terminating the contract would've meant losing any leverage we had over this chappie. We want to retrieve what he's stolen, but if we sack the company, or they sack him, we'll lose any chance of getting the artefacts back.'

There was a logic to that. 'Can I see what's been stolen? Have you got a list?'

Potts fondled his beard nervously. 'We've been trying to compile a definitive list, but he's been very clever at covering his tracks.'

'In other words, you have no idea what he's got away with.'

Potts didn't argue. 'As I say, we've been trying to compile a –'

'A definitive list, yes. So, what's he doing with these pieces? A security guard selling ancient relics is going to raise a few eyebrows, surely?'

'We think he's stealing items to order. Someone else is pulling his strings – someone who either wants these pieces for himself or knows he can sell them on the black market.'

'There's a black market in antiquities?' Even as he asked it, Lincoln knew it was a stupid question. The media was full of stories of ancient sculptures and artworks being smuggled across the world. But did Barbury Museum hold any treasures to equal the ones that hit the headlines? 'Have you told his company what he's up to?'

'We've been waiting to get more evidence.'

'You mean you haven't had the nerve to accuse them of employing a thief.'

Potts didn't argue with that suggestion either. 'It's a delicate situation. It took us a while to realize what was actually missing. Some items simply seemed to have been moved around. At first, I thought our lady volunteers were putting things back in the wrong place when they were cleaning them, but then it was obvious that certain items had actually disappeared. I had to grovel,' he added wryly, 'after doing our volunteers a disservice.'

'Volunteers like Marjorie?'

'Exactly. They're very dedicated, but they're of an age when the brain isn't as sharp as it was. The memory goes.' A helpless shrug.

'Still, they don't cost you anything, do they, so you'd rather not employ younger people who might do the job better.'

He bristled. 'Our budget's very tight. As I was saying, it's taken us a while to work out which guard was on duty at the relevant times.'

Lincoln sighed. 'Give me his name and we'll get him checked out. Chances are, the company didn't do any proper background checks. What's his name?'

'Gomez. Adrian Gomez. He lives on the Barbury Down estate.' Melvyn Potts sniffed. 'That should've been warning enough, shouldn't it!'

Lincoln didn't reply.

10

Trish put a plate of pasta down in front of him, the cheese topping crisp from being reheated. Lincoln had been late getting back after hearing about Adrian Gomez's sideline at the museum and hadn't thought to call her to let her know he'd be home later than planned.

'Actually, I *prefer* cheese when it's burnt,' Kate remarked, looking up from her homework.

'So do I, but I think your mum's trying to make a point.'

Trish sat down opposite him and opened a bottle of wine. 'You wanted to ask me something when you phoned?'

He chewed the pasta manfully. There was well done and there was chewy; this was the barely edible side of tough. 'You know we had this skeleton turn up at the abbey?'

'The one you thought must be left over from some student prank in 1956?'

'Someone at the museum said your library has all the archaeological records – is that right?' He quietly laid his cutlery down, defeated.

Trish took a sip of wine. 'It depends on what the archaeologists and the archaeological societies donate to us for posterity. We've got loads of papers and photos and journals, but no one's ever gone through it to sort it out. We're just thankful for what we get given. Why? Hoping to find sixty-year-old snapshots of some students laying out a hospital skeleton in a rough-hewn grave?' He could tell she was trying not to laugh.

'I wasn't being *that* optimistic.' He helped himself to some wine. He felt he'd earned it. 'So, have you got much about the 1956 dig?'

'Quite a bit. They were hoping to find the tomb of William Spere.'

'The Angling Abbot.'

'I had no idea you were so well up on local history!'

'One of the archaeologists told me all about him.'

'Did she tell you about Saint Aedina of Barbury too?' asked Kate from across the room, without looking up from her tablet.

'Saint Aedina? I've never even heard of Saint Aedina.'

'That's because you didn't go to school round here,' Kate said. 'If you had, you'd have done Saint Aedina to *death*.'

Lincoln had, indeed, not gone to school in Barbury, spending most of his childhood in Worcestershire. If he'd done anyone to death, it was Elgar. 'Tell me about her, then, if you're such an expert.'

'She's meant to be doing her homework.' Trish got up to clear the table.

Kate twisted round in her seat, homework on hold. 'Aedina was a princess – this is, like, a thousand years ago. She founded

Barbury Priory and did lots of good works. Then Lord Harold of Presford sent his soldiers to kill her and he told them to cut her body into pieces and throw it away, so there'd be nothing left to turn into a shrine to her memory.'

The life of Elgar had been much less brutal. 'So why did they make her a saint?'

Kate warmed to her topic. 'After her death, strange things happened. Like a nun who was dying suddenly got better, and a little boy who'd been born blind could see for the first time. People were sure Aedina was working miracles from beyond the grave. And that's why they made her a saint.'

'Did they ever find her body?'

Trish came back in with coffee. 'Anyone would think you were a detective, asking a question like that.' She ruffled his hair as she passed him. 'For centuries, there've been rumours that one of the soldiers, overcome with remorse, went back and gathered up all the bits of her he could find and buried her in secret somewhere in an unmarked grave.'

'Huh! Not sure soldiers in those days did remorse.'

'Another story is that a sick beggarwoman who'd taken refuge at the priory died the same day as Aedina, and somehow the nuns swapped the bodies over. They begged the Abbot to give Aedina's body sanctuary, and that's where she was buried, by night, beneath the walls of the abbey. And yes, I know, that's about as plausible as the first theory, but who knows?'

'So, she could be buried at the abbey after all?'

'If you can believe the story about nuns performing sleight

of hand with a dead beggarwoman, yes, but I don't think anyone takes that seriously these days.'

Lincoln collected some mugs from the worktop. 'Beth Tarrant, the archaeologist, didn't say anything about Saint Aedina.'

'She probably belongs to the "unmarked grave" school of thought.'

Across the room, Kate put on a portentous voice. 'The curse of Saint Aedina! Like the curse of Tutankhamun – whoever finds Aedina's tomb will *die*!'

'Ka-ate!' Trish glared across at her daughter as she poured the coffee.

'Was there some sort of controversy about the 1956 dig? A volunteer at the museum implied something happened.'

'It wound up early, abandoned because bad weather set in – although there were also rumours of a row between Alfred Lever and Paul Roper-Reid. One of them threw his toys out of the pram and flounced off, and by the time he'd pulled himself together, it'd started to rain and didn't really stop.'

'Bit of a wash-out, then.' Lincoln reached for the sugar bowl, visualising something out of *Raiders of the Lost Ark*. He wondered which of the two archaeologists was more like Indiana Jones.

'They found plenty of tiles and pottery,' Trish went on, 'and the sort of rubbish that monks chuck down drains. It's all there in the museum. But they didn't find a single grave, saintly or otherwise.'

'You don't think of archaeologists as being temperamental, do you?'

'Not really. So, what's your archaeologist like?' She peeped at him over the rim of her cup. 'Pretty?'

'She doesn't look much older than a student herself. She's got her hair in plaits with beads in.'

'Not exactly Mortimer Wheeler, then.'

Kate looked up. 'Who?'

'Before your time,' said Lincoln. 'And mine.'

Trish punched him on the arm. 'You want to see what we've got on the 1956 excavations?'

'Thanks, but it's not my top priority, after everything else that's happened in the past couple of days.'

While Kate went up to her room, Lincoln and Trish took their coffee out onto the steps that led down to the garden. The traffic noise from the road was deadened here and, although the railway ran along the backs of the houses a couple of streets away, it wasn't close enough to be a nuisance.

'Two of my cases have collided in a way I wasn't expecting.' Keeping his voice low, he told her how the victim in a violent domestic assault was allegedly stealing from the museum, where another assault had taken place.

Trish pulled her wrap more closely round her against the chill of the evening. 'D'you think there's a connection, or is it just coincidence?'

'Too soon to say.' He stared down the garden into the darkness. 'By the time the bloke from the dig was attacked, Gomez was in hospital, so it can't have been him.'

'Gomez wouldn't have been working alone, would he? Who's told him what to steal? Who's selling it for him? Did your volunteer from the dig see something he shouldn't have?'

Lincoln thought back to Greg Baverstock's room, with its view of one of the museum's fire exits – the one through which Adrian Gomez slipped a couple of nights before the attack.

'Possibly.' He drained his mug, stood up. It was getting too cold to sit out here. He held his hand out to Trish to help her up. 'I'll have to talk to Gomez tomorrow, see what he's got to say for himself.'

11

'What do you mean, he's too sick for visitors?' Lincoln tried to stand his ground against the nurse who was turning him and Breeze away from Adrian Gomez's ward.

She explained that one of his wounds had become infected and, until he was well enough, he couldn't have visitors, not for any reason.

'We could look in on Baverstock while we're here,' Breeze suggested. 'Maybe he's come round.'

But Greg Baverstock was still unconscious, kept in an induced coma until the swelling inside his skull had gone down.

As they turned away from Baverstock's door, a tallish woman in a tracksuit top and jeans came along the corridor towards them from the direction of the drinks machine. She looked about forty, with narrow shoulders and slim hips.

'Are you the police?' She rested her plastic cup on the windowsill. 'I'm Rachel Fielder, Greg's partner. Do you know what happened yet?'

'We're thinking maybe he disturbed a burglar or witnessed a crime,' Lincoln said.

'Some maniac would kill him for that?' She looked tired and

crumpled, as if she'd spent the night beside her partner's sick-bed.

'As I said, we really don't know yet.'

'Then why aren't you out there looking for whoever did this? Greg's in no fit state to tell you anything.'

'When did you speak to him last?' Breeze asked.

'Monday night, about ten-thirty. He was supposed to phone Tuesday night, but when I didn't hear from him, I thought he'd stayed a bit late at the pub and forgotten.' She picked her cup up, sipped from it. Made a face.

'Did he say anything on Monday night about seeing anything suspicious? Anyone hanging around the accommodation block?'

She shook her head. 'He was cross because the dig got stopped. Something about some bones? I mean, isn't that what they were supposed to find?'

'These bones weren't the right vintage,' said Breeze. 'Not nearly old enough.'

She raised her eyebrows. 'I don't know what he gets out of it, quite frankly. You ask him to do a bit of gardening and he can't be arsed. But ask him to dig up a few bones somewhere and he's there with his tongue hanging out. This is his first proper dig, though. He was so excited.'

Lincoln smiled, sympathetic. 'These other digs he's been on – did he ever bring any finds home with him? As souvenirs, perhaps?'

'Souvenirs?' Rachel banged the plastic cup down on the windowsill. Fawn liquid jolted out of it and ran down the wall.

'Never! He'll take photos of things they've dug up, but he'd never steal anything. He'd be blacklisted if he did that. Life wouldn't be worth living if he couldn't do his digs.'

She looked away abruptly. There was a strong chance Greg Baverstock wouldn't get to do another dig. Ever.

'I can't believe this is happening,' she said at last. 'I ought to go home, but I don't like to leave him here on his own.'

'Is it just the two of you?'

'My kids left home before me and Greg got together, and he lost his son a while back.'

'Is there anyone else we should be contacting? Ex-wife, maybe?'

'She wouldn't care whether he lived or died.' Rachel turned away, began dabbing with her sleeve at the stain on the wall, making it worse. 'She's on the other side of the country, anyway, in bloody Norfolk. Let sleeping dogs lie.'

12

Beth thanked God for small mercies: the weather was fine and the dig could continue. Restarting an interrupted dig was always hard work, like going for a run after several days off. She always worried she'd lost the knack until she got back into her stride again.

With any luck, they'd soon hit the layers of rubble and soil that the Victorians had used to backfill the first excavation of the site. Once she and Josh had set out the perimeter of the lost chapel, they could work downwards until they reached the floor of the crypt, where they were bound to find graves and tombs that hadn't been seen for centuries.

'Must be strange treading in your grandfather's footsteps,' Josh said, turning his baseball cap round so the peak was at the back. His face was tanned, lined from years of archaeology in all weathers.

'I just want to finish what he started. Whatever made them abandon the dig, it must've been serious.'

'Aren't they supposed to have fallen out big-time?'

Beth hated the way Grandpa Alf's memory had become tainted by what sounded like petulance. 'They had very different personalities. Roper-Reid was in it for the celebrity. My grandfather wanted to find the tomb of Abbot William. Even if they wasted time on that grave I found on Monday, I doubt they'd scrap the whole dig because of one stupid prank.'

'Don't suppose we'll ever know now.' Josh picked up his tools. 'I'll send someone from my team over to replace Greg, OK? You need all the hands you can get.' He ignored her protests and strode away.

The morning went well, everyone intent on digging and scraping and carrying away, with only a little chatter between them.

At midday, they broke for lunch. While the others took their sandwiches over to the benches on the far side of Abbey Green, Beth walked round the outline of the dig, trying to imagine what Grandpa Alf would have seen here sixty years ago.

Supposing he and Roper-Reid had found the hoax skeleton after all? They might have been so angry, they sent their student helpers away, leaving themselves with too few volunteers to continue. The whole episode would have proved such an embarrassment, they agreed to put nothing on record and never to refer to it again.

But what an ignoble end to her grandfather's career!

Despondent again, she was about to pour herself the last of her coffee when she heard a shout and a dull thud. Spinning round, she saw people rushing across the grass to where a man lay flat out on the ground, a wheelbarrow upturned beside him. She chucked her cup down and started to run, the beads of her plaits battering her shoulders as she went.

It was Sandy, spread-eagled with his left arm under the

edge of the barrow. He groaned in agony.

'What the fuck happened?' Josh appeared out of nowhere, tugging his gloves off and falling to his knees beside the injured volunteer.

'The barrow tipped over,' one of the girls said as they gently, gently eased the wheelbarrow upright. 'He was sitting on the grass and leaned his arm on the handle and it went over.'

'Did you see where it hit him?' Josh asked.

'I'm here!' Sandy snapped. '*I* can tell you where it hit me. I'm not fucking concussed! It fell on my fucking arm! I think my wrist's busted!'

Beth realized she was so scared, she was holding her breath. Was this dig jinxed? The dodgy skeleton, the attack on Greg Baverstock, and now this accident. They say bad things come in threes...

With Josh's help, Sandy sat up, cradling his arm and biting his lip with the pain.

Beth got her phone out. 'We'd better call an ambulance. You could be in shock, Sandy. Someone needs to look at your arm.'

He put his head down as if he felt faint, nodded, didn't argue with her.

'We'll have to fill out a bloody incident report,' Josh muttered to her while they waited. 'Fucking wheelbarrow! Why would you lean on a wheelbarrow? Any fool knows they tip over at the drop of a hat if they're not loaded properly!' He glared across at the little group huddled round Sandy. 'I thought he was one of your better ones, too.'

'Oh, come on. Something like that could happen to anyone.' She patted his shoulder. 'We can do the paperwork together.'

A paramedic turned up on a motorbike, confirming that Sandy's wrist was almost certainly broken and he'd need to go to A & E at Presford General.

'I'm so sorry, Beth.' He seemed beside himself with guilt as she helped him into Josh's car. 'How could I have been so clumsy?'

'Don't worry. Just get yourself better.' She waved him off. No, it wasn't like Sandy to be clumsy. Greg, yes, but not Sandy. Now they'd both be in Presford General – although with any luck, Sandy would be home again by the end of the day, suitably plastered, his arm in a sling.

And, once again, work on the dig had ground to a halt.

13

The offices of Abercrombie & Hale, the security firm engaged by the museum, were up a metal staircase at the back of what used to be Woolworths in Presford. A bored-looking girl in double denim looked up from her computer screen when they walked in.

'You got an appointment?'

'We spoke to your boss earlier,' said Lincoln. 'He's expecting us.' He and Woody showed her their warrant cards and waited while she pressed a buzzer. A bald man with tinted glasses appeared before them, breathless and impatient.

'The police,' she said, returning her gaze to her computer screen. 'Said you're expecting them.'

In an office hardly bigger than a disabled toilet, Brett Hambrook explained the difficulties of recruiting security guards in the present economic climate.

'They don't want the hours, you see. I won't say we don't check these guys out, but we don't do the full background check for every candidate. Wouldn't be cost-effective.'

'So, you risk taking on thieves?' Lincoln wasn't going to let him off the hook that easily.

'Of course we don't! But if these fellas only tell us half a truth, how are we to know?'

'Where did he work before?' Woody had his notebook at the ready. 'We can ask if other employers had any trouble with him.'

Hambrook fidgeted with the folder in front of him on the desk. 'I don't have that information.'

Lincoln tutted. 'You didn't ask for references?'

'The museum needed someone quickly. Adrian fitted the bill, happy to do the hours, didn't mind working on his own –'

'I bet he didn't!'

'Seemed a reliable sort of chap.'

'They always do.' Lincoln held his hand out for the file, and Hambrook, hesitant, pushed it across. One glance inside and Lincoln pushed it back. 'A bit sparse. Not cost-effective to ask him for his employment history?'

Hambrook showed them out a few minutes later. 'I hear Adrian's picked up some sort of infection. Shelley popped in to see him this morning but they turned her away, said it was too risky.'

'They have to be careful,' said Lincoln. 'Stab wounds can turn nasty.'

Driving back to Barley Lane, he let out a snort of exasperation. 'They're in the security business, for Christ's sake! And they don't check out their candidates' job history!' He thumped the steering wheel.

'Makes you wonder why the museum employed a company like that,' Woody agreed. 'Reckon Melvyn Potts couldn't have done much checking-up. Not exactly top-class, is it?'

'You'd think the museum would put it out to contract, not take the first security firm they found in the phone book!'

'We going to try Gomez again? We still don't know who put him up to it.'

'Assuming we're right about that.' Lincoln swung the car into the police yard. 'We know someone was nicking stuff. Potts says Gomez was the security guard on the nights that stuff went missing. We've put two and two together and made four, but maybe we've been too hasty.'

'Didn't Melvyn Potts recognise him from the CCTV?'

'He said he *thought* it was Gomez, but that's not enough to rule out someone else, maybe *another* accomplice.'

'We need someone who knows about the market in stolen antiquities, someone who'd know if anything unusual had surfaced recently.'

'We need Potts to tell us what's missing first. We don't know whether we're looking for an Iron Age burial urn or an Elizabethan necklace.'

'You think they could claim on their insurance? They must have to pay a heck of a premium.'

'If Melvyn Potts's choice of security firm's anything to go by, the museum's contents probably aren't even insured.'

14

Trish was working late at the library, so Lincoln decided to do some work on his house, see what else needed doing that he could get done without taking out a second mortgage.

The garden was a wilderness with a hen house in it and remains of a tool shed. He pushed his way through the long grass to reach the boundary wall, turned and looked back towards the rear of the Old Vicarage. His heart thudded with pride and, if he was honest, apprehension. What had he taken on? Would he ever get it finished?

Small steps, he told himself. One day at a time.

Inside, he went from room to room switching on lights. His domain. His territory. Unbidden, a memory of Cathy returned to him: standing in the living room of their first flat all those years ago, not long after they were married, looking round her, unable to contain her excitement. If she could see him now…

What would she have made of the Old Vicarage? Would she have groaned at the thought of buying somewhere old and semi-derelict? Would she have rolled up her sleeves and got stuck in? If their marriage had turned out the way it was supposed to, they'd have had children by now, be thinking about middle schools and whether she should go back to work…

No. Don't go there.

He climbed the stairs thinking, as he stepped into the box room at the top of the house, how vulnerable he was, the downstairs doors unlocked, the nearest neighbours some distance away, nothing with which to defend himself if he disturbed a burglar here, a vagrant or a squatter. He thought of poor Greg Baverstock, blundering along the corridor in the dark, heading for his room with no inkling of the danger awaiting him.

Then he remembered that fragment of terracotta pottery he'd picked up off his floor. Supposing Baverstock was Gomez's accomplice or even his fence? Had Baverstock got himself onto the abbey dig so he'd be staying next to the museum, conveniently placed to receive the items Gomez was stealing? Had Gomez decided to eliminate him after a falling-out, perhaps?

Lincoln phoned Barley Lane, got Pam, about to knock off for the day. 'Greg Baverstock. What does he do for a living?'

She sounded surprised by the question, so he quickly explained his reasoning.

'I'll check,' she said. 'I'll call you back.'

The trill of his phone in the empty box room sounded as eerie as an owl in a forest. 'Yes?'

'He's a maths teacher at a school in Warminster. Nothing remotely connected to the antiques trade.'

'Damn. Thanks for checking, anyway.'

He was going down the stairs a few minutes later when his phone rang again. 'Pam?' But it wasn't her, it was Presford General, phoning to tell him Adrian Gomez was dead.

15

By the time Lincoln and Pam got to see Gracie at the remand centre, she'd had several hours to process the news that her partner had died in hospital. She wore a bleak expression, her eyes full of despair as she contemplated a future that had, overnight, become quite hopeless.

'He wasn't that ill,' she kept saying. 'I don't understand.'

What charges would she face now? Lincoln wished he could reassure her, but he couldn't. Gomez had died as a result of one of his wounds getting infected, but was that Gracie's fault? A decision would have to be taken but, thank God, not by him. He'd be seeing his boss, Stan Barker, as soon as the results of this afternoon's autopsy were available, and he could ask him then what he thought.

Pam pushed a polystyrene cup of tea towards her. 'Adrian was a security guard, wasn't he?'

Gracie's face was blotchy with crying. She put her hands round the cup, but didn't drink. 'With Abercrombie's, yeah.'

'Did he talk much about his work at the museum?'

'He hated it at first, thought it was a bit creepy, all those dead birds and skeletons and that. It would've given me the willies. He was gonna ask them to give him somewhere else but then…' She stopped, brushed tears away. 'He come home one day, said they'd offered him extra cash if he'd stay on, because nobody else'd do it.'

'How much extra?' Lincoln asked.

'Another eight hundred a month.'

He glanced across at Pam. That would have nearly doubled his salary. 'He ever bring anything home with him?'

'How d'you mean? You asking me if he was nicking stuff?'

Pam leaned forward. 'You can't get him into trouble now, Gracie. You may as well tell us what he was up to.'

Gracie put her head down on her hands, mousy roots showing along her parting where the henna was growing out. When she lifted her head up again, her face was wet with tears. 'I loved him. I didn't mean to kill him!'

Pam sat back. Lincoln crossed his arms. Waited.

At last, she stopped crying and wiped her nose on the back of her hand. 'Some fella put him up to it, some posh git.'

'What was his name?' Pam passed her a tissue and she blew her nose.

'He never said. He'd tell him what he wanted him to nick, and Ade, the stupid twat, did as he was told.'

'He ever mention a man called Baverstock? Greg Baverstock?'

She shook her head.

'You ever see any of the things Adrian nicked?' Lincoln guessed that none of the items could have been very large or else someone at the museum would have noticed they were missing straightaway. 'Did he bring them home?'

She shook her head again. 'This fella waited in his van, took the stuff off him the same night.'

'You called him "some posh git",' said Pam. 'What did Adrian tell you about him?'

'Didn't tell me nothing. I heard his voice a couple of times on the phone, that's all. He sounded posh. Loud and posh.' She said it with a sneer. 'The sort that always gets some other poor fucker to do his dirty work for him.'

'We need to search their flat,' Lincoln said as they drove back to Barley Lane. 'Gomez may have hidden things there without Gracie knowing. What happened to his phone? The posh git's number should be on there.'

'Probably not under "Posh Git", though.' She grinned across at him. 'His phone's probably still in the flat, too.'

'Let's hope we can pick up Posh Git's van on any cameras near the museum. Check that out when we get back. Get Breezy to help you.'

'I can manage on my own.'

'Look, I know you and Breezy don't always get on, but while Graham's on leave, I need you to work together. The sooner we trace that van, the sooner we can make an arrest. And if you think Breezy's difficult to work with, try working with Superintendent Barker.'

'He's retiring next year, isn't he, the Guvnor?'

They got out of the car, headed indoors. 'If he doesn't have a coronary first.' Not that Barker exerted himself much now, counting the days until Barley Lane closed down and Park Street nick took over – not a prospect to which Lincoln looked forward with much enthusiasm. He nodded at the clock as they went into the CID room. 'Gomez's autopsy should be underway about now.'

'I almost feel sorry for Gracie.' Pam dumped her bag on the desk.

'Well, don't.' Dennis Breeze looked up from his screen. 'I've had his wife on the phone, the mother of his little girl, wanting to know when we'll be releasing the body. Nobody'd told her there'd have to be a PM.'

Pam shrugged. 'Not much of a husband, was he, messing around with all those women? Not much of a father.'

'How about that CCTV?' Lincoln reminded her before she and Breeze got into an argument. 'Find out who was driving that van.'

16

Trish shunted the trolley out of the lift and across to the table where her customer was waiting, his phone and laptop bag at his elbow.

'Wow,' he said, 'I wasn't expecting this much material!'

'This is everything we've got in our basement about excavations at the abbey.' She began to unload the boxes of papers onto his table, a sense of déjà vu after her conversation with Jeff only a couple of evenings ago. 'But, of course, the collection's nowhere near complete. I'm afraid you'll find lots of gaps.'

'There's way more stuff than I could've hoped for. Thank you!' With deft, suntanned hands, he grabbed the first box and flipped the lid open, pulling out papers and photos, drawings and newspaper cuttings.

'Are you involved in the dig?' Trish slid the last box onto the table.

He grinned. 'One of the archaeologists and I are old friends.' He spread out a couple of pages from a magazine dated 1883: *Oxford academic uncovers abbey secrets of a thousand years ago.* The grainy photograph showed excavations as messy as the aftermath of a car-boot sale. 'Those Victorians sure knew how to destroy a site!'

He folded the magazine up and began to sift through the next box of papers. 'St Aedina of Barbury,' he said, holding up a newspaper cutting so fragile it looked ready to fall apart. 'She isn't buried here, is she?'

Trish took the cutting from him, making a mental note to photocopy it before it disintegrated. It depicted a somewhat idealized image of Aedina looking like a Hollywood starlet of the 1930s, along with a photo of the abbey. 'Probably not. No one knows for sure. Funnily enough, my daughter and I were talking about her only the other night.'

'She must be quite a local heroine. Aedina, that is, not your daughter!' His smile made Trish melt a little inside. She guessed it was meant to. She tried to place his accent – American? Canadian?

'Most people round here don't know much about her beyond the myths they're taught in school.' She leaned on the handle of the trolley. This man seemed to radiate sunshine she'd be happy to bask in till the end of the afternoon – a much more appealing use of her time than totting up the quarterly enquiry statistics. And yet...

'Myths?' His eyebrows went up. 'Such as?'

'That she performed miracles after she was murdered – which is probably no more than a tall tale passed on by travellers to get a drink or a bed for the night.'

'But *based* on fact, surely? Most myths are.'

'Maybe, but the lines get muddled. Where does fact end and fable begin?'

From the next bundle of papers, the man unfolded a large

engraving, extracted from an eighteenth-century book on the town and its environs. It depicted a church-like building, mostly in ruins, open to the sky, with ivy romantically entwined around its broken pillars. The legend read *Barbury Priory, famed for its martyr, St Aedina.*

He smoothed the engraving flat. 'How about this priory she founded? Is it far from here?'

'About three or four miles, but it's long gone, destroyed soon after her death. Bits of the building turned up in local houses for decades afterwards, apparently, townspeople salvaging the stones and timbers and reusing them. No one even knows for sure where it actually stood.'

He looked disappointed. 'And no one knows where she's buried?'

'You should find an article in one of these boxes, about her body being taken to Barbury's sister priory in West Wales, near St David's, but that's just speculation.'

'So, St David's is what – two hundred miles from here?'

'About that, yes.'

'Wow! That's a long way to take a body.'

'I suppose we'd all like to think she was buried with dignity somewhere, rather than being chucked away like an animal carcass, but how can you prove anything like that after so long? The poor woman's bones could be scattered all over the place between here and Cardigan Bay!' She straightened up and began to wheel the trolley away. 'I should let you get on with your research.'

'That's OK – it's good to talk to someone who knows about the history of this place.'

'Will you be working on the dig yourself?'

'I'll be dropping by later to see how they're doing.'

'They had a bit of a hold-up. One of the team got attacked and ended up in hospital. I know the policeman who's leading the investigation,' she added, when the man looked surprised.

'Guess he can't tell you too much, though, huh?'

'Not really, no.' She'd already said too much, decided it was time to get back to her enquiry stats. 'Let me know if you need anything else.' The wheels screeched as she shunted the trolley away.

Back at her desk, Trish thought what a difference it would have made if Aedina had been buried in Barbury. The abbey would have become her shrine and drawn pilgrims from all over England, all over Christendom – at least until the Dissolution.

She worked on the enquiry statistics, trying to make sense of the figures her assistant, Briony, had scribbled down. Was that a one or a seven? A seven or a nine?

The spreadsheet completed, she found herself searching the internet for St Aedina, curious about why the experts now thought she was buried near St David's. At last she found why the Welsh had laid claim to Barbury's very own saint.

Twenty years ago, a metal detectorist field walking in West Wales found a small object that appeared to be part of a matrix or seal possibly a thousand years old. After months of research, historians declared it was from the matrix of St Aedina: a wyvern, like a tiny dragon, ensnared by a letter A.

A matrix, Trish knew, was a stamp used to authenticate

documents. When pressed into wax, it left a unique imprint as binding as a signature. Upon Aedina's death, it would have been broken up and thrown into her coffin to signify the end of her earthly power. If so large a fragment had turned up in a Welsh field, it must prove her coffin reached the sister priory near St David's after all, and that the gory stories of her body being torn limb from limb were simply that: gory stories.

Trish skimmed the article, learning that the sister priory now housed a St Aedina Visitor Centre and an Aedina Healing Waters Retreat.

A rustle of papers, the woody aroma of expensive aftershave, subtly applied: the man had come into Trish's office. She'd been so absorbed, she hadn't heard his approach.

'I guess I've seen all I need to right now. Thanks for your help, Miss –?'

'Trish. Trish Whittington.' She scrambled to her feet, flustered. 'Yes, if there's anything else you need, you know where to find me. Us. The library.'

He grinned and sauntered off, his laptop bag under his arm. She rather hoped she'd see him again.

17

The sun had come out at last, making the grass sparkle all around them. Dressed for a chillier day, Beth began to sweat as she clambered in and out of the trench, carting barrowloads of soil across and tipping them onto the tarpaulins, then wheeling the barrow back again. Nobody talked much, concentrating on their various tasks. She took photos as she completed each stage, determined to leave a more comprehensive record of the excavations than her grandfather and Paul Roper-Reid had.

On her knees, brush and trowel in hand, she felt a shadow cast across her. Sweeping a forearm across her damp face, she looked up and –'Troy!'

Troy Benedict was standing above her, hands in pockets, smiling down. 'Hi, Beth!'

'I thought you were still in the States! You should've told me you were coming!'

'I wanted to surprise you. How's it going?'

'Slow but sure.' She sprang to her feet and pulled her gloves off. 'The full extent of the crypt's beginning to emerge.'

'Crypt? What crypt?' He grinned. 'Just kidding. I'm impressed!'

She climbed out of the trench and stood beside him so she

could point out the area she and her team had uncovered during the past few hours. 'And down there,' she told him proudly, jabbing with her trowel, 'on that side, as close to the river as he could be buried, I just *know* we're going to find dear old William Spere.'

Troy pulled a handkerchief from his breast pocket and wiped it across her forehead. 'Dirty girl.' He chuckled as he showed her the hanky, streaked with mud. 'So what's so special about William Spere? Aren't there any other abbots just as worthy of investigation?'

She laughed too, thrilled to have him around at last. 'Call yourself an expert? I thought you'd be sure to know! They didn't just bury Abbot William in the grave – he's supposed to have been surrounded by gifts from the Prioress at Barbury Priory and from abbots of all the abbeys in Wessex!'

'What happened to "We brought nothing into this world, and it is certain we can carry nothing out"?' He seemed highly amused. 'What kind of gifts?'

'That's what we'd like to find out! Probably nothing precious like gold, but the historical implications of seeing those treasures…!'

'You're searching for buried *treasure*?' Now he was winding her up.

'Historically speaking. Ecclesiastically speaking.' And she was teasing him back.

And then another shadow spread across the grass: Josh, striding over with his spade to see why she'd stopped work.

'Everything OK?' He lifted his baseball cap, scratched his head, pulled the cap on again.

Beth pushed her visitor forward. 'Troy, this is Josh Good. Josh, this is Troy Benedict, the guy I told you about that I met at uni.'

Josh ignored Troy's outstretched hand. 'I hear you're a bit of an expert on this period.'

'Yes,' said Troy, 'I made early ecclesiastical history my specialty. I've published papers, done some broadcasts, been lecturing for a few years now, so – yeah, I guess you could say I'm a "bit of an expert". And I've started work on a book.'

Josh sniffed. 'If you've come all the way from the States to help out, we ought to find you some tools – but you might want to change into something more casual.' He swung his spade onto his shoulder.

Beth could've clouted him for being so offhand. All Troy wanted to do was give them a bit of encouragement, yet here was Josh, behaving like a little boy defending his den against a kid he doesn't know.

Troy shoved his hands in his pockets again, still amiable. 'I'm happy to leave the heavy lifting to you guys. Just wanted to see how Beth's dig is shaping up.'

'It isn't *Beth's* dig.' Josh planted his feet apart. 'We work together.'

'Oh, for fuck's sake!' She shoved him so hard he nearly fell over. 'If Troy can help, then let's use his expertise, not get into a pissing contest!'

Troy seemed more amused than offended. 'Look, let me buy you guys a drink later and we can talk this through some more. I'm staying at The Black Swan. Why don't you join me there at, say, six-thirty?'

Beth watched Josh's face, willing him to say yes. At last he took his gloves off and put his hand out for Troy to shake.

'Six-thirty, then,' he said. 'Who knows, we may have found a few graves by then.'

18

The Guvnor's office at Park Street police station always reminded Lincoln of his headmaster's study: devoid of clutter except for a couple of dull ornaments on the desk or windowsill that inevitably drew the eye while harsh words clattered round the room.

Chief Superintendent Stan Barker had a face like thunder, though Lincoln guessed chronic indigestion was as much to blame as the Adrian Gomez case.

'This Bell woman.' The Guvnor cleared his throat and wiped his mouth with a yellowish handkerchief. 'Come across her before, haven't we?'

'Yes, she's been on the receiving end in a couple of domestics – most recently when her flat got set on fire. She was lucky to get out alive.'

'Was that Gomez?'

'No, the one before.'

The Guvnor wagged his balding head. 'Do they never learn, these women?'

'Do any of us?'

'Huh! We need to make sure we've got everything together

for the CPS. Might've known this sort of thing'd happen, my last few months.'

'Sir?'

'I'll be finishing end of the summer, early autumn. My post will go and they'll start to run things down at Barley Lane. Don't look so shocked, Jeff. You knew it'd happen sooner or later. My retirement gives them leeway to make it happen sooner, that's all.'

The Guvnor was right. Lincoln knew it would happen, but now it could happen this year rather than next. He tried not to let it worry him.

'We've been looking into allegations that Gomez was stealing from the museum, Sir.'

'Is that worth pursuing now the fella's dead? Things are pretty tight, as you well know. The thieving's bound to stop now, surely?'

Lincoln didn't share his boss's optimism. 'Gomez wasn't working alone. Whoever put him up to it, they may not want to stop.' He explained about the security firm employed by the museum, the laxity of the background checks on their guards. 'Whoever it is, he'll want to find someone else to take Gomez's place. I've got officers looking for cameras that might have picked up a van we think was involved.'

The Guvnor looked fed up. 'The museum's reported these thefts? Officially?'

'The Facilities Manager's putting something together for us.'

Barker coughed again and the custard-coloured hanky reappeared. 'Bit arse-about-face, isn't it? Doesn't he already know what's missing? How does he know he's being robbed if he doesn't even know what's been taken?'

Lincoln shrugged, keen to get out of his boss's office and back to Barley Lane. 'Probably embarrassed that he's handed his security over to a bunch of crooks.'

A search of Gracie's messy flat had yielded nothing that looked as if it had been nicked from the museum – indeed, nothing that looked as if it had been nicked from anywhere. Gomez must have been told what to steal and then passed the items to his accomplice the same night without bringing them home. Disappointingly, his phone wasn't in her flat either, which seemed a bit odd.

'Can I ask what Gracie's going to be charged with now that Gomez has died?'

The Guvnor made a face, as if her fate was of little interest to him. 'Murder, probably. If she hadn't stabbed him, he'd still be alive.'

'But the wounds weren't deep – more like lacerations than stab wounds.'

'That's for the legal bods to sort out.' He picked the report up, dropped it again. 'As far as I can see, Jeff, she grabbed a knife and went into the bedroom fully intending to attack him with it. If he hadn't died, that'd be wounding with intent. She wasn't defending herself, was she?'

'No.' Poor Gracie had been through a lot, but no one could justify her launching an attack on Adrian Gomez when she caught him in bed with another woman. 'She could get life, couldn't she?'

The Guvnor pursed his lips, considering. 'Depends whether the jury feels sorry for her. Either way, I'd better get on to the CPS, get things moving. If there's nothing else –'

His computer beeped with an incoming message and he glanced at the screen, his question unfinished. 'Good God!' He reached for his handkerchief again, blowing his nose like an elephant trumpeting. 'The results of the Gomez post-mortem. Cause of death was asphyxiation. Says here he was *suffocated*.'

'Suffocated? You mean, someone killed him?'

The Guvnor slowly lifted his gaze as if his eyes felt heavy in their sockets. 'God only knows what that does to the Bell woman's case!'

'Those stab wounds wouldn't have been fatal.'

'No, but if she hadn't stabbed him, he wouldn't have been anywhere near that hospital.'

Lincoln's mind raced. Gracie hadn't wanted her lover out of the way, but somebody else did. The man he'd been stealing for?

Barker heaved himself to his feet. 'Pointless arguing about this now. Get back to Barley Lane and find out who killed him. At least you know your Mizz Bell has got a cast-iron alibi.'

19

Beth stared disconsolately at the clothes draped over the sofa in her apartment. What had she brought with her that was smart enough for The Black Swan?

Come on, Lillibet – it's a drink in the bar, not a slap-up meal in the restaurant! Wash your hair, put a bit of make-up on, white blouse, black denims.

Why did her mother's voice always intrude when she needed a bit of a talking-to? Why had they more or less stopped talking to one another over the past few years, behaving more like old schoolfriends who've grown apart? Was it too late to get her mother back?

'You look nice,' said Troy, turning from the bar at her approach. He looked rather crisp and well groomed himself: chinos, an olive-green shirt open at the neck, a pale linen jacket. Hard to believe he hadn't long stepped off a plane and driven down from Heathrow.

'I nearly came along in my work clothes,' she confessed. 'I didn't think I had anything remotely sophisticated enough for this place!'

The Black Swan was now Barbury's swankiest hotel,

centuries old but recently refurbished for a more discerning clientele than the gentleman farmers and army wives who used to be its main customers. It had retained the Victorian grandmother clock and plush velvet banquettes in the entrance lobby, but the old wallpaper had been replaced with matt emulsion in shades of taupe, aubergine and chalk.

Troy's eyes scanned the bar. 'Josh not joining us?'

'He should be. He probably went home first. Maybe his wife wouldn't let him come out again.'

'Like that, huh?' He chuckled as he hailed the woman behind the bar.

'They've had a few problems.' Beth stopped before she betrayed any confidences. 'How long are you over here?'

'What are you having? Wine?'

'Cider, please. Organic, if they've got it.'

They took their drinks over to a table in the window, one that only had two seats, she noticed. When Josh turned up, he'd have to nick a chair from a neighbouring table.

Troy set his phone down beside his glass and leaned back in his seat. 'So – you think you've found Abbot Spere's grave?'

'I've mapped the extent of the crypt. If the contemporary accounts are to be believed, he should be against the wall nearest the river bank. We just need to keep digging away until we get down to floor level.'

He held his glass under his nose, inhaling the wine fumes for a few seconds before taking a sip. 'I've been reading up about that saint that was martyred here.'

'Aedina?' Beth gulped back some cider. 'Why the sudden interest in Aedina?'

'I've been kinda fascinated by her story for a while now, all the contradictions, all the arguments –'

'Arguments?'

'Over whether she's buried here or not.'

'Nobody knows. She was said to have been torn limb from limb and thrown into the River Press or some Wessex wood.' She dumped her glass down, wondering where Josh had got to. He knew more about Aedina than she did. 'Another story is that some contrite soldier salvaged what he could and carried her remains to Wales.'

'Near St David's, yes.'

She sensed something, a question – or maybe an answer – lurking beneath his reply. 'Have you found something in the literature? Troy?'

When their eyes met, she couldn't look away. She hadn't noticed before the unusual colour of his: green, hazel, amber under dark lashes.

'I may have stumbled on something.' He leaned close to her, his voice low. 'Something that doesn't seem to be in the published literature.'

'Josh is the man to ask. He did his doctoral thesis on Aedina and her priory.'

He sat back, surprised. 'Did he now?'

'He's been planning a book for ages but he's so busy with fieldwork and the day job, God knows when he'll get round to it!'

Not to mention trying to keep his marriage together.

'Maybe we could collaborate.'

She laughed. 'Not sure either of you is suited to that sort of arrangement.'

'Isn't archaeology all about collaboration? Teamwork?' His eyes shone, mischievous. 'The guys who worked on the abbey in the 1950s fell out over it, didn't they? Roper-Reid and Lever?'

Should she tell him about Grandpa Alf? Or did he already know about her family connection? 'No one's really sure what happened. Only that the dig was cut short and they all went home. The records are sketchy.'

'You must have a theory. You'd have been crazy to follow in their footsteps without checking out the problems they ran into.'

'Naturally, if we thought they'd abandoned the dig on safety grounds – unstable soil conditions or evidence of contamination by disease or something – but there was nothing in the records.'

'You said the records are kind of sketchy.'

'Yes, but surely if they'd found something bad, they'd have recorded it?'

'Absence of evidence isn't evidence of absence.'

'Oh, for fuck's sake, Troy!' How could he sit there so smugly, talking to her as if she were still that first-year student at Exeter and he the golden boy brought back to inspire the freshers. 'They were seasoned professionals, both of them! I've got all Alfred Lever's personal stuff so –'

'You have?'

Bugger. The cat was out of the bag. 'He was my grandfather,' she said at last. 'Everything he didn't donate to the Bodleian, he passed on to my mother, who passed it on to me.' Which wasn't entirely true. Beth couldn't be sure she had *everything,* since her mother had been steadily "jettisoning ballast", as she put it, over the past few years. 'I've got anything of any significance.'

Troy let out a low whistle. 'Kind of a dark horse, aren't you, Miss Tarrant?'

'It wasn't like I was keeping it a secret. It simply isn't relevant. I've been interested in the abbey since long before I knew my grandfather led the dig here in '56.'

'OK, so why do you think they abandoned the dig, if it wasn't on the grounds of safety?' He sipped his wine, his eyes on her face all the time.

'I don't know. Nobody knows. Clash of personalities, probably, a storm in a teacup. Roper-Reid was always a bit of a grandstander.'

'So they say.' Troy put his glass down, empty. 'I'd love to take a look at Lever's papers. Do you have them here in Barbury?'

'The most relevant material, yes. It's all back at the flat.' She caught sight of a baseball cap going by the window. 'There's Josh.' Annoyed that he'd turned up after all. Annoyed with herself for being annoyed.

Josh stood in the doorway, his eyes screwed up as they adjusted to the dimness of indoors. As he caught sight of her and Troy, he snatched the baseball cap from his head and crammed it into his anorak pocket.

'This one's on me,' said Troy, getting up and striding across to the bar. 'What'll it be?'

20

More trawling of CCTV tapes, this time from the hospital, looking for anyone acting suspiciously in the vicinity of Adrian Gomez's ward.

'This is bloody hopeless.' Breeze snapped open another packet of nicotine gum. He'd been trying to give up smoking, but Pam knew he was having a hard time of it. 'People are in and out of there the whole fucking time.'

They'd agreed to share the boring task of checking the footage around the time of his death, but Breeze was right: the camera filmed all the comings and goings through the main doors into the ward, so they'd simply have to watch to see who might have diverted their footsteps into the side ward where Gomez was lying.

'OK, Dennis. Just look out for anyone who shouldn't really be there.'

They looked, they paused, they looked away to give their eyes a break.

'This Gomez bloke was sick, wasn't he, going septic where he was stabbed?' Breeze sucked his gum noisily. 'How do we know for sure he was murdered?'

'You can tell from the eyes.' Pam watched as a porter made

several vain attempts to manoeuvre an empty trolley through the swing doors. Eventually a nurse left her station to go and help him, exchanging a few words and patting him good-naturedly on the back as he steered the trolley off down the corridor and out of camera range. 'Petechial haemorrhaging, a classic sign of asphyxiation. All it takes to kill someone is a pillow or cushion held down over their nose and mouth for a few minutes.'

'Fighting for breath.' Breeze groaned. 'Bastard way to go. Make mine quick so I don't see it coming.'

'Hang on – I know that man!' Pam jabbed her screen and he craned round. She'd spotted a wiry figure shouldering his way into the ward, certainly not a member of staff. In jeans and T-shirt, his jacket half on and half off because his arm was in a sling, he sidled across out of shot, in the direction of Gomez's ward.

Together, counting the minutes, they watched.

'Four minutes forty seconds,' Breeze said as the man re-emerged. 'That'd be long enough to hold a pillow over somebody's face.'

'It's that Scottish guy, the one who found Greg Baverstock after he was attacked.'

'Just unlucky, is he, blokes he knows getting attacked?'

'Or he's had something to do with it. Sandy McFarlane,' Pam remembered. 'One of the volunteers on the dig.'

'So, he puts a sling on to look like he's been to A & E and then wanders round like he's looking for the exit?'

'It worked, didn't it? He got as far as Gomez's ward without being challenged.'

'Is the time right? Is that when Gomez was killed?'

Pam checked the autopsy report Lincoln had put on her desk before he and Woody went off to the museum. 'There's a one-hour window between nurses checking on him, and it's round about then.' She picked her phone up eagerly. 'I'd better give the boss a ring, tell him the good news.'

'Your Mr Gomez has died,' Lincoln said when he and Woody were seated across the desk from Melvyn Potts.

'*My* Mr Gomez?' Potts tugged at his beard. 'Hardly.'

'The man who was systematically stealing artefacts from your museum, then. Him. He's dead.'

Potts shifted his gaze from Lincoln's face to Woody's, as if seeking moral support. 'That's unfortunate. Adrian was a bit light-fingered, but he wasn't an unpleasant chap. I hadn't realized he was so unwell.'

'He wasn't. Someone murdered him.'

'I thought he was still in hospital.'

'He was, but someone didn't want him coming out again.'

'You're saying someone killed him because he was stealing from the museum? Surely that's not worth killing for?'

'Depends how much those items are worth.' Lincoln held his hand out. 'How about that list you were putting together?' He didn't expect to get it.

'Actually...' Potts dived forward and started tapping away on his keyboard. In the corner of the office, a printer chuntered and whirred, one, two, three pages churning out of it. They watched until it went quiet and Potts got up to retrieve its output.

Lincoln skimmed through the list, handing each sheet to Woody as he finished it. The items seemed unconnected: a gold armlet from Central America, studded with turquoise; three antique spice jars believed to be from the West Indies; a mah-jong set dated 1712...

'Do these things have anything in common, apart from no longer being in the museum?'

Potts gave him a sour smile. 'Apart from being relatively small, these are all items that were donated to the museum a number of years ago. None of them's ever been on the market before.'

'Meaning?' Woody patted the sheets together and handed them back to Lincoln.

'Meaning it'd be hard to put a price on them.'

Woody sniffed. 'Reckon they're only worth what someone's prepared to pay for them.'

'Isn't there an issue of provenance?' Lincoln said. 'If they've never been on sale before, how would a buyer know they were getting the genuine article?'

A shrug from Potts. 'Whoever put Adrian up to it must've known he could sell them or he wouldn't have asked him to keep taking things.'

There was a logic to that but the randomness of the items troubled Lincoln. Wouldn't collectors want artefacts that met certain criteria, that fitted in with what they already had?

'What about insurance?' asked Woody. 'Are you able to claim on what's gone missing?'

Lincoln noted the sheepish look on Potts's face. 'The items *were* insured, weren't they, Mr Potts?'

'Of course, but I was hoping we'd get them back somehow! I hadn't put a claim in yet, but if Adrian's not coming back…'

Lincoln took a photo from his folder and laid it on the desk: a black van caught on camera on Sunday night, the same night Gomez was taking boxes away from the museum. 'Any idea who that vehicle belongs to?'

Potts frowned at it. 'That's right outside the accommodation block.'

'We think it was waiting for Adrian Gomez to come out of the museum with his latest haul of antiquities. Have you ever seen it before?'

Potts glanced at Lincoln as if he feared it was a trick question. 'Never – although one black van looks much like another. Who does it belong to?'

Lincoln slid the photo back into his folder. 'We don't know yet.'

The one camera that had picked up the van was at West Gate House, home of a solicitor called Shiner and his family, and was at the wrong angle to pick up the number plate. The only distinctive feature was a sticker in the back window, depicting possibly a tree in leaf, a large flower or a mushroom cloud – it was too far away to make it out.

'You think the driver of the van is a likely candidate?'

'No honour among thieves,' said Woody.

Lincoln stood up. 'Who upped Gomez's salary? We heard he

was offered more money to stay on here.'

Potts spread his hands, absolving himself. 'That must've been the people at Abercrombie's. *I* certainly didn't.'

'Reckon we could trawl back through the West Gate House CCTV,' Woody wondered, 'see if that van shows up last week, say?'

He and Lincoln were walking back to the car, neither of them satisfied that Melvyn Potts was being straight with them.

'Pam and Breezy thought of that, but the Shiners only keep a few days' worth then record over it. The Shiners hadn't noticed the van, but then, why would they? As our friend Melvyn said, one black van looks much like another.'

Across Abbey Green, Beth Tarrant and her team seemed to be digging down deeper than ever. The litter of trays, plastic water bottles and abandoned equipment reminded him of school outings when they'd stop for a picnic and leave everything lying around until one of the masters bollocked them to clear it up.

'Let's see how they're doing.'

Before Woody could object, Lincoln had loped across the grass towards where the young archaeologist was hard at work, her beaded plaits flicking up and down as she worked.

'If you've come to see if we've dug up any more bones we ought to have told you about…' She squinted up at him, hands on hips, her nose and arms sunburnt.

'Just wondering where you've got to.'

'Come down and see for yourself.'

Once he was in the broad trench beside her, Lincoln could get a sense of what this space was. He could even make out a few worn stone steps, winding in a spiral but going nowhere. 'You've been busy since I was here last!'

She couldn't hide her excitement. 'This part of the abbey was excavated in the 1880s but never properly preserved or recorded. We assume the team who found it took out what they wanted and filled it in again. The dig in 1956 was meant to uncover it and excavate it properly, but they ran out of time before they got very far.'

'Because of the prank skeleton?'

She shook her head and her plaits rattled. 'I still don't think they found it – there's nothing on record. I only wish their notes were more complete!'

'You've been to the library to see what Trish Whittington's got?' Woody asked. Trish was his wife's sister so he was as proud of her, in his own way, as Lincoln was. 'She might be able to *dig up* a bit more for you.'

Beth rolled her eyes. 'I'd be surprised if the library's got anything I haven't already seen but, yes, perhaps I'll go and look later today.'

'Wait till Monday,' Lincoln said. 'Trish isn't on duty until then. You've got someone to replace Greg Baverstock, I see.' He nodded towards a man he didn't know, tall and dressed more smartly than the other volunteers, digging away at the other end of the trench.

Beth looked pleased. 'Oh, that's Troy Benedict. He's especially interested in this period. He's a university lecturer in the States, but he was desperate to take part in our dig.'

'That must be the bloke Trish met yesterday,' Lincoln said as he and Woody walked back to the car. 'Seemed quite taken with him.'

'Bit smarter than the chaps on *Time Team*.'

'*Time Team*?'

'You should get yourself a television, boss. Not that it's on any more, except on the Yesterday channel. What d'you reckon to Melvyn's list?'

'The items seem such a weird assortment – all different ages and nothing in common.'

'Except they're all missing.'

'There is that, yes.' Lincoln checked his mobile. 'Damn! Pam's been trying to get hold of me and my phone was off.' He called her, listened while she told him Sandy McFarlane had gone into Gomez's ward around the time he was killed.

'I'll get an address for him,' he told her. 'Then we'd better pay him a visit.'

21

'Aye, I was at the hospital getting my wrist fixed.' Sandy McFarlane lifted his arm up to show them his impressive navy-blue cast.

Breeze nodded in sympathy. 'I did my ankle a couple of years back. Still gives me gyp when the weather's damp. I tell you, I –'

'How did you break your wrist, Mr McFarlane?' Lincoln asked, although Beth had already told him when he asked her for the volunteer's address.

'Bloody barrow tipped over, right onto my arm. Clean break. Could've been worse.' He patted the cast, looked up again. 'Aye, I thought I'd look in on Adrian while I was there.'

'You and Adrian Gomez were friends?' Lincoln guessed the two men were roughly the same age, early forties, McFarlane slightly the older.

'Not so much friends as family. My sister's married to Jim, whose brother Jon's married to Lina, Adrian's sister. Adrian's my brother-in-law's brother-in-law.'

Lincoln couldn't even begin to work that one out. 'Did you talk to him? I'm surprised they let you into his ward. We were told he was off-limits while he was infectious.'

'I didnae ask anyone, to be honest. Nobody stopped me.'

Lincoln and Woody had called on McFarlane at his bungalow on the edge of Barbury. It was gradually being surrounded by a new estate of townhouses that seemed brash and out of scale there, and the looming presence of a gigantic electricity pylon only fifty yards from his back gate must have cast a bit of a blight on its value too. Not that a huge pylon had deterred the developers.

The bungalow might have looked drab from the outside, but inside, it was full of light and – Lincoln couldn't help noticing – artworks and antiques that must have cost McFarlane a bob or two. As he scanned the room, he noticed metal security grilles concertinaed back behind the curtains, not quite out of sight: common enough in London houses but rarely installed in Barbury bungalows.

'You working?' Breeze asked.

'Between jobs. My sister and me, we had a shop in town, fabrics, wool and what-not, but it went to the wall a few years back. And of course,' he added, gazing across at the view through the French windows of cranes and pile drivers, 'I was taking care of our mam. Suited me to run a couple of part-time jobs so I could spend time with her, but after she passed, I felt I deserved a wee bit of time to myself.'

'You live here on your own?' Lincoln surveyed the large sitting room, wanting McFarlane to know he'd clocked the Chinese vases, the silver candelabra and the Victorian water colours.

'I prefer it that way – although,' and he lifted his cast up ruefully, 'there's times I could do with a bit of help.'

No one said anything. One of his several clocks chimed,

not quite on the hour. Breeze crossed his legs, left ankle on right knee, the sole of his desert boot white with chalk dust from the unmade-up road that, for now, led only to McFarlane's front gate.

Lincoln said, 'You must be wondering why we're here.'

The Scotsman's mouth broadened into a sarcastic grin. 'I may be a skinny wee Scot who left school with only a handful of qualifications, but I'm not stupid. Adrian was murdered, I know that. And you're going to tell me now I was the last person to see him alive. Isn't that right?'

'That's right,' said Breeze, jiggling his foot.

McFarlane lifted his arm up yet again. 'And how'm I going to murder a man when I've only got the use of one arm, eh? Can you tell me that?' He got to his feet, the plaster cast clutched across his stomach. 'And why in God's name would I kill him? He's *family.*' As if that mattered.

Lincoln stood too. Compared to him, McFarlane was indeed a "skinny wee Scot" though with his weight behind him he could easily have pressed a pillow over Gomez's face for as long as it took for the life to go out of him.

'Did you see anyone else around Adrian's ward when you were there, apart from the hospital staff?'

'I didnae see a soul apart from the nurses.'

'What did he say to you?' Breeze asked. 'What did Adrian say?'

A one-shouldered shrug. 'Asked me what I'd done to myself, told me he couldnae wait to get out. We promised ourselves we'd go for a drink when he got home.'

Home? Lincoln thought of Gracie's wreck of a flat. Was

Gomez planning on going back to his wife and daughter? Or did he have somewhere else?

'Where was home?' he asked with an urgency that seemed to take the Scotsman aback. 'Where did he mean, "home"?'

'He's got a wee house…He *had* a wee house off the London road, along near the crematorium.' McFarlane wrestled his smartphone from his pocket, thumbed through his contacts until he found Gomez's address. 'The woman next door's got a spare key.'

22

Rachel Fielder couldn't stay at the hospital indefinitely. There'd been no change in Greg's condition but, as the doctor said, that wasn't necessarily bad news. Let the swelling subside, let him begin to heal, and they'd bring him out of his coma. If they could. The doctor hadn't spelled it out, but he hadn't needed to. She wasn't naïve enough to expect Greg to snap awake and be right as ninepence.

She went home to a house that was subtly altered. Greg's belongings, the daft things he'd pick up on beaches and bring back from walks – the driftwood, the little toys kids had dropped and not gone back for, the foreign coins, the scraps of broken Wedgwood he'd found on the edge of a ploughed field – had taken on a sadness, a pointlessness, ranged along the mantelpiece and the edges of bookshelves.

She made the bed and washed up, but the walls were closing in on her, so she changed into her running gear and drove to Shearwater. The lake, not far from Longleat, was like a flat pewter disc that afternoon, its surface hardly ruffled by wind or birds or even fishermen although, as always, a few of them were sitting on the bank.

She ran with long, loping strides along the path and under the trees, stopping to get her breath back, stiff after several days not running.

That's how they'd met, she and Greg, here at Shearwater, nearly four years back...

She'd been jogging along, oblivious, when a black Labrador had come hurtling out of the undergrowth across her path. How she hadn't gone head over heels, she'd never know, but somehow she'd sidestepped the dog in time, crashing instead into the big, bluff man who'd charged out of the undergrowth after it.

They both ended up on the ground, Rachel on top of the man, the dog bounding round them, panting.

'Bloody hell! You should have him on a lead!' She was on her hands and knees, checking she hadn't broken anything.

'He *was* on a lead but his collar's come undone.' The man rolled onto his side, stood up, then bent forward, winded. 'Sorry.' He straightened up and she saw how tall he was, taller than her, about her age, dark hair going grey, kind eyes. 'Rooney, show this lady how sorry we are.' And at the click of the man's fingers, the dog threw itself onto the footpath, its paws in the air, rolling its eyes.

Rachel just stood there, shaking her head, trying not to laugh. 'You've trained your bloody dog to say sorry?'

'I've had to. We're both such clumsy idiots.' He held his hand out – grubby, grazed – and she took it. 'Greg Baverstock.'

'Rachel Fielder. You ought to clean that up,' she added, jabbing at the blood on the heel of his hand. 'Looks like you've got grit in it.'

Six months later, they'd moved in together. A couple of months after that, Rooney got knocked down by a car and Greg decided he wanted to move somewhere else. They got a house together on the edge of Warminster and life moved on. She tried to make the place homely, but there was something missing, something missing in Greg.

It was only months later that he brought himself to tell her he'd had a son, Rory, who'd died after some playground accident when he was fourteen, a football hitting him on the head in one of the several places where, they discovered afterwards, his skull was especially thin.

Greg's marriage fell apart after Rory's death. His wife remarried and moved away, and only his job as a teacher kept him sane, he said. He'd drifted until that day at Shearwater when he crashed out of the undergrowth after Rooney and crashed right into her.

Now, Rachel stopped and gazed over the shimmering water. The leaves were coming properly into leaf. It would soon be Easter, usually her favourite time of year. But not this year.

She started to run again, her mind whirring, whirling her back to the hospital room where Greg lay inert, helpless. She listened to her feet pounding, then heard another sound, other feet, someone behind her, someone catching up to her, faster paces, shorter legs, their feet hitting the footpath in a weird kind of syncopated rhythm. She glanced across to see a young man, a boy, haring along beside her, his face obscured by the hood of his sweatshirt.

Was he chasing her? She slowed and so did he. She stopped and he went on running before turning and running back.

'You Rachel?'

Bizarrely, she wondered if he'd come from the hospital, a messenger they'd sent to tell her something had happened to Greg. Then she realized how stupid that was.

'Who wants to know?' She stepped back away from him, weighing him up: seventeen, eighteen? Very short fair hair, a bony face, a tattoo on his neck, a leather thong like a choker at this throat. He wasn't as tall as her, would be no match for her unless he had a weapon. He looked like the sort of youth who'd carry a weapon...

'What happened to Mr Baverstock? Is it true he's in hospital?'

'You know Greg?' Was this one of his students? Christ, surely not! She kept glancing at his hands, scared he was about to reach for a knife.

'Is it true? Has someone hurt him?'

'Someone hit him over the head, yes.' She rose up on her toes, ready to take flight if she needed to. She had a sudden memory of Rooney who, eventually, learnt how to run with her without tripping her up. What wouldn't she give to have Rooney here! To have Greg here! She felt tears welling up.

'Is Mr Baverstock going to be OK?'

'Do you know who did that to him? It wasn't you, was it?'

Alarm filled the lad's face, hardening his mouth. Then, as quickly as he'd appeared, he spun round and sprinted back the way he'd come. Before Rachel could catch up with him, he'd leapt onto a motorbike parked under the trees near the tea rooms, and sped off.

Her heart was thumping, her knees were shaking. Who was he? What did he want?

As she chucked her running shoes into the boot of her car, she spotted a scrap of paper on the ground near where the motorbike had been parked. It was a page printed off her garden centre's website: a group photo of all the staff, their names printed underneath. There she was on the end of the middle row, grinning like a fool above the uniform polo shirt and tabard. Her face had been ringed round and round in Biro.

She felt as if someone had pinned a target on her.

23

'Smells like Burger King round here,' Breeze remarked as he and Lincoln walked up to Adrian Gomez's front door. The narrow terraced house was indeed very near the crematorium, and the pungent odour of burning wasn't entirely imaginary.

As Sandy McFarlane had said, a neighbour had Adrian's spare key.

'He hasn't lived here in ages,' she said sourly when she came back from fetching the key from her kitchen drawer. She told them her name was Kylie, like the singer. 'But he's always popping in and out. Or was. Can't say I'm surprised the way things have turned out. The whole family's bent.'

'Really?' Lincoln and Breeze exchanged glances. 'In what way?'

'Con artists, the lot of them. His sister used to sell dodgy stuff down the market. I mean, everyone knew they were fakes, but to hear Lina talk, you'd think she got hold of the real deal through someone she knew in London and she was doing you a big favour letting you buy it cut price.'

Breeze took the key from her and began to edge towards Gomez's door. 'What sort of dodgy stuff?'

'Clothes and bags. Those shoes with the red soles. Old pictures, china, vintage furniture about as vintage as I am...' Kylie winked at Breeze. 'I heard she pushed off to Spain a while back, does all her trading on the internet. Listen, pop back when you're done and I might find you a cup of tea.'

Gomez's house smelt musty, like old newspapers and empty milk cartons. A tom cat had come in not long ago, spraying its trademark scent around before it left.

'Gomez has been using this as a store,' Lincoln said, surveying the stacks of brown boxes like the ones they'd seen him carrying out of the museum, each one about the size of a cake box. 'Just how much has he got away with?'

'How long was that list the museum bloke gave you?'

'Three pages, about sixty items.'

'There's a lot more than that here.'

'How did he know what was in any of them? They're not even labelled!"

'One way to find out.' Breeze produced a Swiss army knife from a clip on his belt and, placing one of the boxes on the dining table, on top of a tablecloth spattered with stains, he slit it open.

When he lifted the lid of the box, a tangle of shredded paper rolled out. In a nest of straw inside sat a terracotta figure, small but bulbous, featureless, its hairstyle suggested by long lines drawn in the clay, with more lines suggesting drapery that only partly clothed it.

He hooted in disgust. 'It's a little fat lady! Who the fuck'd want *that* on their mantelpiece?'

Lincoln picked the figurine up, cradling it in the palm of his hand where it fitted, warm to the touch. 'There's another one like this at the museum. It's a Venus figurine.'

Breeze frowned at it. 'Worth anything?'

'The one at the museum's thousands of years old, so I imagine it would be.'

'So, the museum had two? The one you saw and this one?' Breeze opened another box with a swift stroke of his penknife. Shredded paper oozed out when he lifted the lid. He pushed the straw back and eased out another burgeoning Venus. 'Or three? Did the museum have *three*?'

'They're fakes.' Lincoln set down the Venus he'd been holding. 'Gomez was stealing stuff from the museum so someone could copy them for his sister to sell. For all we know he wasn't even *stealing* a lot of the items – he was borrowing them then putting them back when the copies had been made. That's why Melvyn Potts couldn't be sure what was missing. Things would disappear and then turn up again.'

'Or,' Breeze said, opening yet another box and taking out yet another Venus, 'Gomez kept the original and put a copy back in its place.' He grinned wickedly. 'Neat, eh?'

24

The CID room was stuffy and everyone looked keen to go home. Lincoln wished he had better news for his team, but at the end of a long day, he seemed to have more questions than answers.

'So, what have we got?' He uncapped a marker pen and started to scribble on the whiteboard. 'Adrian Gomez was stealing items from the museum and taking them out through the fire exit to someone waiting in a black van. The room where Greg Baverstock was attacked directly overlooks that fire exit.'

He pointed to the relevant images on the board.

'Now, when Baverstock was beaten up, Gomez was already in hospital so *he* wasn't the attacker. But we also know from Gracie Bell that Gomez was working with someone she called Posh Git, on account of his voice. My guess is, Posh Git wanted to make sure Baverstock couldn't tell anyone what he saw from his window.'

'Isn't that a bit extreme?' Pam was doodling in her notebook, a sure sign she was uncomfortable with Lincoln's assumptions. 'Wouldn't they have tried to find out if Greg was really a threat before setting out to murder him? It's a bit of an escalation from stealing museum exhibits to killing someone.'

'Yes, but what Gomez was stealing could've been worth

thousands. When there's big money at stake, a man can become ruthless enough to kill anyone who gets in his way.'

She didn't seem convinced, but Lincoln needed to move on.

'Gomez had two strings to his bow,' he said. 'Stealing valuable exhibits at the behest of Posh Git, and passing other items on to his sister, Lina Cox, so she can sell rip-off versions on the internet. His house is chock-a-block with boxes of reproduction antiquities.'

He stuck Lina's Facebook profile photo on the whiteboard. She didn't look like a woman you'd mess with.

'The only suspect in the murder of Adrian Gomez is Sandy McFarlane – except we haven't any proof. He broke his wrist earlier in the day and his arm was in plaster – that's why he was at the hospital. Did he break his wrist on purpose, to give him an excuse to be wandering around the wards, or was it a lucky accident – who knows? Either way, no one apart from nursing staff went anywhere near Gomez around the time he was murdered.'

'But why would McFarlane want Gomez dead?' Woody asked.

Breeze chuckled. 'You should see his house! Something of a collector, is our Mr McFarlane. I bet he's got contacts in the antiques trade. He sounds too Scots to be Posh Git but he could be his go-between. Gomez isn't much use to Posh Git now he's in hospital, is he? Could even be a bit of a liability. So Posh Git gets McFarlane to make sure he's out of the way.'

Lincoln scrawled POSH GIT on a sheet of A4, provoking a murmur of laughter when he stuck it in the middle of the board.

Whoever this man was, he was crucial to all these crimes.

'Would Lina Cox know who Posh Git is?' Pam wondered.

'If we could track her down.'

Not long before the briefing, Lincoln had spoken to Sue Gomez, Adrian's widow. The two women had fallen out several years before, Sue said, over which of them should look after the elderly Mrs Gomez, and they hadn't spoken since. Sue was sure Lina spent most of her time in Spain now, especially since husband Jon had gone off with a woman half Lina's age.

'Did Adrian know anyone who spoke in a posh voice?' Lincoln had asked her.

'No. We never moved in them sort of circles.'

Now it was Woody's turn to seem unhappy. 'Counterfeit antiques are a matter for Trading Standards, aren't they, not us. Shouldn't we be letting Trading Standards go after Lina Cox?'

He was right, and the Guvnor would probably say the same if he was here. Lincoln stood there, marker pen in hand, sensing a mutiny.

'Helping his sister fake pottery goddesses is one thing, Woody, but Gomez was also stealing valuable items for whoever this Posh Git is who was pulling his strings. And that *is* a police matter, isn't it?'

'Can I just say…?' Pam's cheeks coloured. 'The attack on Greg Baverstock. I still don't think…'

She ran out of steam, glaring at her notebook. Then, just as Lincoln was about to say something, she lifted her head up and interrupted.

'I think we should look into Baverstock's life a bit more. You're assuming he was attacked because of what he might have seen at the museum, but it doesn't feel right. Supposing he's fallen out with someone who's taken advantage of him being away from home, no security, a little bit drunk?'

What was Lincoln always telling his team? Never assume – and he'd done just that, leaping to the conclusion that Baverstock was silenced because he'd seen Gomez stealing from the museum. He hadn't really considered any other motive for the attack.

'Good point, Pam. You're right. We need to look into his personal life, any problems, any conflicts. Talk to Rachel Fielder, see if she can tell you anything.' He caught her eye, keen to make sure she knew she'd done the right thing by contradicting him, uncomfortable as it was for both of them. Their eyes met and she looked quickly away, her colour rising again.

'McFarlane,' said Breeze, putting his feet up on the seat of the empty chair in front of him. 'Why don't we go back to him, tell him what we know about the thieving, see how he reacts?' Lincoln noticed that the soles of Breeze's boots were still chalky from his previous visit to McFarlane's bungalow.

'Good thinking. It's too late to call on him tonight, but first thing in the morning, catch him early, get him on the back foot. You and me, Dennis, OK?'

Breeze grinned. 'OK by me, boss!'

Mutiny averted.

25

Beth padded up the stairs from the bathroom, leaving damp footprints on the carpet. All she wanted to do was slip under the covers and catch up on some sleep.

Her phone rang as she was pulling on the top and jogging bottoms she wore for bed. Troy? Why was he phoning now?

'Have I caught you at a bad time?' He sounded apologetic even before she'd said anything.

'I was about to turn in, actually.'

'It's twenty past nine. What are you, ten years old?'

She couldn't help laughing. 'It's been a long day and I can't fucking sleep in this place for all the silence!'

'You and me both. Shall I come over there?'

'What? Over *here*? You don't know where I'm staying.'

'Oh, but I do! And I'm right outside your door, so if you're going to send me away, at least give me a cup of coffee first.'

They lounged on the sofa, drinking wine and snacking on nuts and the gluten-free nachos she'd brought with her from London in case Barbury didn't have any.

'I think I know what started the row between Roper-Reid

and your grandfather,' Troy said, holding a nacho up to the light as if considering its artistic possibilities.

'You do?'

'Roper-Reid wanted to excavate that north-south grave you found on Monday, but Lever thought it was a distraction.'

'And how do you figure that one out?'

'I've come across a journal article – something that Roper-Reid wrote some time afterwards, where he says that, in 1956, he was "denied the opportunity to investigate the tantalising prospect of a pre-Christian burial on the site of the abbey's western chapel." That's the grave that *you* found, isn't it? "Denied the opportunity" – guess you could read all kinds of meaning into that phrase!'

How could she have missed that reference? She'd been so fixated on her grandfather's writings, she'd skimmed over most of what Roper-Reid wrote – including the article Troy had discovered.

'It sounds as if they found it after all,' she agreed, 'but decided against excavating it.'

He smiled and dropped his arm across her shoulders. 'Maybe they simply ran out of time and hoped to come back to it the following year, if they could get the funding.'

Was Troy being too kind to Grandpa Alf's memory? 'You think Roper-Reid was keen to dig and my grandfather said no?'

'Don't blame your grandpa. You're doing a dig, you have parameters and you stick to them. You have a deadline, you have objectives. Even in 1956 I guess they had objectives.'

'Bloody management-speak.' She and Josh had been obliged

to complete a multitude of applications for grants and bids for funding, ticking the right boxes so whoever was paying them knew what they were paying them to do. Back in 1956, the same pressures were there, even if they were described in a different vocabulary.

Troy pulled her closer. 'More wine?' He leaned across her to pick up the bottle and top up their glasses.

'Please. How long are you here for, in England?'

'It's a whistle stop. I fly out Tuesday.'

'Tuesday? But that's only a couple of days away!'

'I'm right in the middle of something back home. I've really gotta get back.'

"Back home". Was England no longer home to him? She sipped her wine, enjoying the weight of his arm across her back, the warmth of his hand on her upper arm, his fingertips not quite brushing her breast.

'So what papers of your grandpa's do you have here?' He took his hand away, sat up.

Beth plonked her glass down and padded over to the wardrobe, conscious of his eyes on her. She hauled her briefcase out and tipped a couple of folders onto the coffee table.

'These are his plans.' She'd got them on her tablet, but it was so much easier to spread them out on the floor and let Troy marvel at them the way she'd marvelled the first time she'd seen them.

He was lost for words, his eyes widening. 'Wow!' he said at last. 'These are unbelievable!'

On hands and knees, they explored the plans, working out how they aligned with Beth and Josh's excavations, noting the differences, pointing out what was still to be uncovered.

'And what's this?' Troy pointed to a fuzzy part of the diagram, the only section that wasn't meticulously drawn and inked. 'Any ideas?'

Beth peered closer, unable to make out the tiny handwriting, in Grandpa Alf's exquisite copperplate, beside the apparently unfinished section on the edge. 'This is roughly where William Spere should be,' she realized at last. 'Only it looks as if there's another grave next to it.'

Troy sat back on his heels. 'Is that possible?'

'Abbot William's as close to the wall of the crypt as they could put him. There's no room for another grave next to his.'

'Could it be it's a grave outside the chapel walls?'

Beth sat back too, stunned. 'We didn't pick anything up on the survey.'

'Surveys can be misleading.'

'Only because they give you too much noise, like water pipes and buried cables. They don't usually miss something like this.' And there was no budget left to bring the survey equipment back.

'Come on,' said Troy, getting to his feet with the ease of an athlete. 'Put it all away for now. We won't come up with the answers tonight.'

'But whose grave do you think that might've been?' She'd never sleep now. Even as she was folding up the plans and slipping them back into her briefcase, she was imagining herself unfolding them tomorrow morning down on the site, early, no one else about, trying to line everything up so she could make sense of it.

'Some cleric less distinguished than your Angling Abbot, obviously!'

'A cleric buried outside the chapel walls? I don't think so!'

'Maybe I can help you find out tomorrow, OK?' He took the briefcase from her, slid it carefully onto the shelf of the wardrobe. 'Make an early start, many hands make light work, blah blah blah.'

As he turned back from the wardrobe, he reached his arms out to embrace her, to pull her close.

'Troy, I –' She put up her hands to push him away, but instantly gave in, letting him fold her into him and carry her across to the bed.

26

'So, what,' said Breeze, 'we tell him we know about the figurines, ask him what else Gomez was up to?'

Lincoln opened the car window a few more inches. Breeze must have dined on curry last night. Curry and lager and the only cigarettes he allowed himself all week. 'That'd be a start, Dennis, then see what else he knows. Could be it's McFarlane who's been advising his brother-in-law's brother-in-law what to steal, but who's Posh Git?'

When they left Barley Lane, they'd had to squeeze through several pillars of brown cardboard boxes brought in from Gomez's house. Lincoln prayed that Trading Standards would take them off his hands in the morning, especially now he was sure he could detect a faint odour of tom cat about them. Then if Trading Standards wanted to pursue Lina Cox and her lucrative line in fake Venuses, they were welcome.

Now Lincoln and Breeze were heading back to Sandy McFarlane's bungalow. As they approached, the electricity pylon loomed overhead, somehow more obtrusive and monstrous at this time of day, the morning sunshine glinting off its massive legs. Was it humming? Wasn't it bad for you, living near a pylon?

They pulled up outside. The security grilles were across the windows, the curtains drawn. All around, the building site was deserted, not even a guard dog patrolling.

Lincoln led the way up the path. No sign of life. 'Must be having a lie-in.'

'Most people do, Sunday morning.' Breeze belched and Lincoln looked away.

McFarlane didn't come to the door when they rang. Lincoln peered through the letter box but the hallway was too dark to see anything. He thumped on the door. Breeze pulled up McFarlane's number and rang it. They listened.

'Phone's ringing inside.'

Breeze went round to the side door, called out to say it was open and he was going in. The next thing Lincoln heard was a bellow, before he saw Breeze charging out again, a hand over his mouth, reaching the garden fence in time to vomit copious amounts of liquefied curry into the flower bed.

They stood by the car, watching blankly while the SOCO team took over.

'Looks like he put his head in a freezer bag.' Breeze treated himself to a steadying cigarette. 'Must've decided he'd had enough.'

Lincoln watched Sandy McFarlane's body being slid into the mortuary van. One black van looks much like another, he thought, but some look blacker than most.

'Yesterday, did he seem like a man who'd had enough?'

Breeze shrugged, smoked, tapping his ash back into the packet. 'No sign of forced entry. Not that I had time to look around...'

'Did he leave a note?'

'Like I said, I didn't have time...'

Lincoln patted him on the shoulder. In a minute, he'd put his protective gear on, go inside and take a look for himself. One thought dominated the rest: how does a man with a broken wrist put a freezer bag over his head and tape it shut one-handed?

He looked away over the top of the car, breathing in the scents in the morning air: cows a couple of fields away, grass, cement dust, diesel. He wouldn't have had Sandy McFarlane down as suicidal.

The pylon was definitely humming.

27

The sound of church bells churned up the Sunday-morning air between the abbey and the houses all around it.

Beth squinted out through half-open eyes, the bedroom flooded with sunlight filtered through lace curtains. She pushed the covers back, saw she was naked, remembered with a rush of terror that she'd spent the night with Troy. Terror because she *never* spent the night with anyone she knew as little as she knew Troy, even though they went way back.

She peeped over her shoulder to see if he was still beside her, but the bed was empty, the sheets hardly disturbed. She hadn't *dreamt* it, had she?

Her head was thick with wine, her nose stuffy, her throat sore. This was the morning she was going to rise early, explore the site on her own before anybody else was up. Fucking half past ten!

She got up anyway, skipped breakfast, drank some soy milk, packed some nachos in a box and headed out. Why hadn't he stayed? Breakfast with Troy would've been fun.

Joggers were making a circuit of the abbey grounds, while an elderly Chinese woman was leading a tai chi class under the trees, the grass spangled with dew. Beth felt a stab of guilt at the messiness of the excavations, the way they'd torn an ugly gash in the otherwise pristine lawns.

Who else might be buried inside or next to the crypt, and why hadn't she noticed that unidentified location on Grandpa Alf's plans? Trust Troy to expose her oversight, to home in on the one bit of the site map she hadn't studied properly! Trust Troy to steal a march on her, finding that article by Roper-Reid – though it still didn't explain why the dig was halted the way it was.

She resolved to visit the library tomorrow, talk to this Whittington woman, see what material she might have that Beth had never seen or even known about. She strode across to the trench, confident that despite losing two volunteers, they'd soon be able to see what tombs and graves lay beneath the rubble that was left. She was about to take a couple of photos with her phone when she heard Josh calling her. He came loping across in his Sunday best, not looking like Josh at all.

'I've had the police come round,' he said grimly. 'They tried you first, but your phone was off. Sandy McFarlane's been found dead.'

'Sandy?' She put her phone away, the photos forgotten. 'How? What happened?'

'Suicide, apparently, or so they think.'

'Suicide? Sandy?'

'They couldn't say much.' He hovered, keen to go, probably due in church, his wife waiting. 'You OK? You look a bit –'

'Yeah, I'm fine. It's a shock, though. Sandy? Really?'

'See you tomorrow.'

'Yeah, tomorrow.' She felt dazed, unable to process the news. Then Troy turned up, bright as a button, sauntering across from The Black Swan, intent on taking her for brunch somewhere and wanting to know what was up.

28

Rachel Fielder seemed glad of an excuse to get outside. 'I don't like leaving him,' she said to Pam as they took the stairs down to the garden at the back of the hospital, 'but I'm going stir crazy.'

It was chilly, even though the sun was trying to shine through, but Rachel didn't seem to mind. She took a couple of cereal bars out of her shoulder bag and offered Pam one.

'Not very healthy,' she said, 'but they plug a gap.'

Pam thanked her and peeled the cellophane from a sweetened concoction of dried fruit and pressed wheat. 'Tell me about Greg.'

They sat on a bench between some pampas grass and a cheery forsythia.

'Not a lot to tell. What you see is what you get.' Rachel must have realized how unhelpful that was because she apologised and began again. 'He's a kind man, a bit naïve in some ways, always sees the best in people. He's been teaching for years and seems to love every minute of it. And in the holidays, he loves scratting around in trenches. On the downside, he doesn't open up a lot. We'd been together for ages before he even told me he'd got a son – *had* a son – who died.' She bit into her cereal bar.

'How long ago did his marriage break up?'

'Seven years or thereabouts. She treated him horribly, considering all they'd been through.'

'Losing a child...' Pam looked away, trying hard to imagine what it must be like to be a parent and then to not be. Or maybe you always were, even if the child was gone. 'Was there anybody else?'

'Did his wife have somebody else, d'you mean?'

'No, did Greg? Before you.'

Rachel posted the last of the cereal bar into her mouth, her cheek bulging. 'He went a bit wild, or so he says. Went on the internet, met all sorts of strange women.'

'That's not how you two met –?'

'Christ, no! But...' Rachel screwed up the empty cellophane, then opened it out again and smoothed it across her knee. 'He's had a few flings since we've been together. Nothing serious, nothing I've ever felt threatened by but...' She halted, stood up, the cellophane consigned to her pocket. 'I think one of the women was still married.' She suddenly seemed to realize why Pam was asking. 'You think a jealous husband came after him? That he was hit over the head and nearly killed because he got involved with somebody's *wife*?'

'Unless you can think of any other reason why Greg was attacked.'

Rachel shook her head. 'I always knew something bad would happen if he started messing around with married women.'

'Do you know her name, this woman?'

'No. We agreed not to talk about it. I hated him screwing

around, but if he was going to do it, I didn't want to know the details.' She thought for a moment. 'She'd be on his phone.'

'We didn't find his phone.'

'No, of course not.' She looked more downcast than ever. 'You take so much for granted, don't you, when things are going OK? Then something like this happens and you could kick yourself for not appreciating what you've got.'

'Shame it takes something like this to teach us that.'

They began to walk back indoors.

'Me and Greg, we rub along, comfortable with each other, y'know, never saying what we feel. I should've valued him more.'

Pam had already turned away, heading for her car when Rachel called after her.

'He backs up his contacts to his laptop. I'll check when I get home, if it's still working. I'll know her name when I see it.'

29

'Don't know why people collect all these knick-knacks,' said Woody. He'd come to Sandy McFarlane's bungalow so Breeze, still feeling dodgy, could go back to the station.

'It's all about aesthetics,' Lincoln said. 'And some of these knick-knacks, as you call them, are probably worth a small fortune. You noticed the security grilles?'

'What's he do for a living if he can afford this sort of stuff?' Woody ran his hand over a rosewood side table that looked earlier than Victorian.

'He told us he was between jobs after his fabric business went bust. Looks as if he lived pretty modestly otherwise.'

The equipment in the kitchen was functional but old-fashioned, probably purchased by his mother, who must have been the original owner of the bungalow. As he gazed out over the building site surrounding it, Lincoln wondered if McFarlane had been holding out for a good price from Finnegan Property Development, who'd surely love to knock the bungalow down and bury it under another half-dozen townhouses.

'Reckon he didn't live here on his own all the time,' Woody

called out from the bathroom. 'Two cabinets like me and Suki have got at home.'

'What, like his 'n' hers?' Lincoln went to see.

Woody opened both cabinets, one either side of the shaver point and mirror. The left-hand one contained Sainsbury's men's deodorant, shaving foam, toothpaste and shampoo. In the right-hand one were decidedly more expensive toiletries that even Lincoln knew were top of the range, by Floris and Penhaligon's, and a badger-hair shaving brush from Trumpers.

'This is more what you'd call "his 'n' his",' he said with a laugh. 'Now we need to find out who McFarlane's house guest was.'

30

Greg's laptop didn't want to come on. Rachel sat hunched over it at the kitchen table, willing it to work, but it refused to co-operate.

The blue screen of death, she'd heard him call it. It must have been mortally wounded.

She left it while she raked through a plastic crate of papers that he hadn't got round to sorting, probably never would now. She whisked through Post-It notes, index cards, pages off jotter pads, searching for anything that would help her identify the woman he'd been sleeping with before Christmas.

Last year's diary! She dived onto it, flipping through the pages, back and forth, pouncing on anything that looked relevant.

And there she found it, on 21 December last year: Anna Preston. A mobile number. A pub in the High Street, 7.30.

She was about to text Pam Smyth the details when she stopped herself. Anna Preston. She knew who that was. Her husband, Wayne, was a tree surgeon. They lived out in one of the villages off the A36, but he worked all over the place – Barbury, Presford, Fordingbridge.

She looked him up on her phone, found a photo of his workshop right next to his house. Drove out there, parked in a lane that snaked round the village, strolled past the house which was at the top of a long, sloping field. A low-powered motorbike was parked on the forecourt of the workshop, two lads in hoodies bending over it with oily fingers, trying to fix something, oblivious. She recognised one of them.

That lad had been trying to tell her something at Shearwater, she guessed. But what?

She pretended to make a phone call, snapped the boys, the bike, the house and workshop. Strolled back to her car and drove home.

31

'We found a name in McFarlane's paperwork,' Lincoln told the team as Sunday drew to a close. 'Henry Clyde.'

'And who's Henry Clyde when he's at home?' Breeze had recovered his usual ebullience and was tucking into a crusty roll he'd nabbed from the canteen before it shut.

Lincoln consulted his notes. 'Early sixties. Dealer in antiquities and fine art. Cautioned a few years ago for receiving stolen goods – he must have convinced us he didn't know they were stolen. Antiques showroom in Presford. Looks as if he lives over the shop.' He picked up his phone. 'Let's give him a ring.'

If he hadn't already worked it out from the grooming products in McFarlane's bathroom, Lincoln knew as soon as he came on the line that Henry Clyde was Posh Git. His accent was so upper class, he made English sound like a foreign language.

'Mr Clyde, can we talk about your friend Sandy McFarlane?'

A long, slow-breathing pause. Lincoln half expected him to hang up. Then, 'What do you want to know? Is something wrong?'

'When did you last see him?'

'Not for a week or so. He's been staying at the museum

doing one of his digs…' He tailed off. 'Has something happened to him?'

'Might be best if we spoke to you in person, Mr Clyde. You mind if we come round?'

The street windows of Henry Clyde's antiques emporium were masked by gilt security grilles so you couldn't see in, unless, like Lincoln and Woody, you were let in by the owner and escorted through a shadowy jungle of dark furniture and claret-coloured wall hangings to his upstairs flat.

He offered them tea or whisky, but they declined both, keen not to get too friendly with the man Lincoln suspected of stealing from the museum.

Immaculate in blazer and twill slacks, Clyde sat himself down on a chair in the bay window overlooking Shipton Street. The light falling onto his face accentuated his ageing complexion and tinted his unnaturally black hair a radiant ginger. A CD was playing quietly – something baroque that Lincoln couldn't quite place.

'I suppose this is about Adrian, isn't it?' Clyde folded his hands on his knee. 'I saw he'd died.' He nodded towards a tablet computer on the table beside him. 'I shouldn't have got him involved, I realize that now.'

Lincoln played dumb. 'Involved in what, Mr Clyde?'

'Removing things from the museum. Recovering things.'

'Recovering? Not stealing, then?'

'A substantial number of exhibits in that museum belong, by rights, to my family. To me.'

Woody chuckled, humouring him. 'How d'you reckon that, then?'

'My grandfather, Matthew Clyde of Presford Grange, amassed a fine collection of artefacts from all over the world. He had rooms set aside for their display and, as a young boy, I played with African weaponry, musical instruments from Central America, anything of cultural or historical significance. My grandfather instilled in me, his only grandson, an appreciation of aesthetics, of fine arts and crafts, and he promised me, promised me *faithfully*, that when he was gone, I would be the custodian of his vast collection.'

He swung his arm wide, as if to encompass the world.

'I'm guessing that didn't happen,' Lincoln said.

'Sadly, no. My father died before my grandfather did, so my uncle became his heir instead. When my grandfather died, the house and everything in it went to my uncle, who gambled away most of it and gave the rest away to the museum. So, you see, I haven't been stealing anything, simply taking it back.'

'But it's not yours to take, is it, if your uncle gave it away?' Woody pointed out.

'That's a matter of opinion.' Clyde sniffed. 'When I met Adrian and discovered he'd got a job there, well –!' He smiled as if it must be obvious to them that he had no choice but to take advantage of a corruptible security guard.

'How did you meet Adrian?' Lincoln asked, wondering where on earth their paths might have crossed.

'There's a club Sandy and I go to sometimes, a *private* club. Adrian's a member too.'

'And the name of this club?'

'Carew's.'

Carew's was Barbury's only explicitly gay bar, in a cramped old pub down near the railway station.

Woody's eyebrows went up. 'Adrian swung both ways?'

Clyde sneered at the expression. 'If you must put it like that, yes.'

'So, you gave Adrian a list of things you wanted him to take from the museum, then you waited outside to collect them.'

'What? No! He'd put them in the boot of his car and meet me in the abbey car park when he left work.'

Lincoln was puzzled. 'You don't own a black van?'

'No, the shop van's white. You can ask Sandy. He'll tell you the same.'

Lincoln paused, took a breath. 'Sandy was found dead at his home this morning.'

Henry Clyde's whole body shuddered as if a jolt of electricity had been shot through it. 'What? Sandy? But...' He tried to stand but had to sit down again, his legs too weak.

'How did he seem last time you saw him? Depressed? Remorseful?'

'Remorseful? About what?'

Lincoln had to tread carefully. 'We believe he murdered Adrian Gomez.'

Clyde went deathly pale. Christ, that's all they needed, another suspect pegging out! Then he asked for some whisky, pointing to a cut-crystal decanter on the sideboard. Woody obliged, filling a matching glass and passing it across.

'Mr Clyde, was it you who asked Sandy to kill Adrian?'

The look on Clyde's face said it all. 'Of course I didn't! Once he'd recovered, Adrian would've gone back to the museum and continued to help me reclaim what is, by rights, mine. And why would I ask Sandy to do something so terrible?'

Lincoln believed him, even though that destroyed his theory that Posh Git was behind Gomez's murder. Had Sandy acted to protect Clyde, then? Or because he was jealous of Gomez's relationship with him?

He tried again. 'If Sandy thought he'd done a terrible thing, would he want to end his life, d'you think?'

'He wouldn't take his own life!' Clyde banged the flat of his hand against the arm of his chair. 'Someone must've killed him! Does that mean my own life is in danger?'

'I don't know.' Lincoln had little sympathy for him. 'Why would anyone want Sandy dead? Had anyone threatened him?'

'Not as far as I know. How did he –? Did he –?'

'Someone put a bag over his head,' said Woody. 'He was asphyxiated.'

'Oh, God! Where is he? Can I see him?'

'He's at the mortuary. Actually, we need someone to identify him officially. Would you –?'

'Yes, yes.' Clyde covered his face with his hands for half a minute; when he took them away again, he looked refreshed, reset. 'Everything Adrian took from the museum is here, Inspector. I paid him royally because I was so grateful for his help in retrieving my family heirlooms.'

So much for Abercrombie's increasing his salary, as Gomez had told Gracie. Easier to tell her that, Lincoln supposed, than to admit his boyfriend was paying him on the side.

'Can we assume you'll be giving them back to the museum as soon as possible?'

'I suppose it would be the most sensible action to take, wouldn't it?' Henry Clyde smoothed his hair back as if preparing himself to go on stage. 'I'd like to go to the mortuary now.' He stood up, walking stiffly across the room to turn off the CD player and pick up his door keys. 'Would someone be able to run me home again?'

MONDAY

32

The crime-scene photos from Sandy McFarlane's bungalow made a gruesome start to the week. The weather had turned chillier, with rain in the air, just enough to spoil a day out.

'We can discount the black van outside the museum – it was nothing to do with Henry Clyde, so we can stop searching for it. We also know that Clyde wanted the antiquities for himself, not for resale – which didn't stop Gomez borrowing a few other items for his sister to turn into fake *objets d'art*. What we don't know is, who killed McFarlane and why?'

'Reckon he must've known his killer,' Woody said. 'There was no sign of a break-in, so he must have let them in.'

'Any prints?' Breeze asked.

'Nothing on the bag or the tape. The only other prints were McFarlane's and Clyde's. I don't think he had many visitors.'

Pam frowned at the photos. 'Wouldn't McFarlane have tried to grab hold of his killer's hands or wrists when they were putting the tape round his neck? Was there nothing under his fingernails?'

'Nothing. His left arm was in plaster and not much use to him if the killer came up behind him, so he probably didn't get a chance to defend himself.'

'Could it be someone from the gay bar scene, perhaps?' Breeze chomped on his chewing gum. 'Jealous lover? Rent boy taking advantage?'

Lincoln shook his head. Either was a possible motive, but from what Clyde had told them on the way to the mortuary, it was he who tended to "flirt around", as he put it. Sandy was less interested in sex than in having a companion like Clyde who knew his way round fine art and fine wine.

'He was such a name-dropper,' he'd said affectionately. 'He was thrilled to think I'd met Brian Sewell and Roy Strong, and people like the Saatchis.'

'I'm certain Clyde didn't want Gomez dead, but McFarlane may have been afraid he'd tell someone what he'd been up to at the museum. That'd be the end of Clyde's reputation and his business, even if he didn't go to jail. I think McFarlane murdered Gomez to shut him up.'

'Then who killed McFarlane?'

Lincoln scanned the whiteboard, dismayed by the shortage of suspects. A couple of days ago, he'd put Posh Git at the centre of a conspiracy to steal valuable antiquities from the museum and sell them on the black market. Adrian Gomez had been the thief, passing his spoils on to Posh Git waiting in a black van.

Now, that "conspiracy" had degenerated into Henry Clyde's stealthy regaining of property he still considered his own, and Gomez's pilfering of items for his sister to copy and pass off as real.

And in the middle of all of that: Sandy McFarlane.

'And Greg Baverstock?' He pointed to the blurry photo of Greg that Woody had printed off Linkedin. 'What's the latest, Pam?'

'According to Rachel Fielder, he had a fling with a married woman just before Christmas. Could be her jealous husband's caught up with him.'

'Why wait four months to have a go at him?' Although when he thought about the way his own jealousy had simmered after Cathy left him for Andy Nightingale…

He stood poised with his marker pen. 'This woman's name, the husband's name?'

Pam checked her phone then looked up, disappointed. 'Rachel was hoping to get the contact details off Greg's laptop and send them to me, but she hasn't texted me yet.'

'I thought his laptop was fucked.' Breeze looked round at her. 'If she hasn't sent you anything, that's probably why.'

'I'll try her again in a minute.'

'What about the sister?'

Lincoln turned back from the whiteboard at Woody's question. 'Whose sister?'

'Adrian's sister. Lina Cox. Could she have killed McFarlane? If she thought he'd killed Adrian?'

'According to Adrian's widow, Lina's in Spain. She may not even know he's dead.'

Woody shrugged, disappointed. 'Just a thought.'

'Dennis, see if you can get an address or a number for Lina Cox, here or wherever. Woody and I will go to the museum, give Melvyn Potts an update. Perhaps he won't press charges against Henry Clyde if he knows he'll get his artefacts back!'

33

At the library, Trish leafed through the papers strewn on the desk in front of Beth Tarrant. 'I can't understand what's happened to all the stuff on the history of the abbey. This box was full!'

'But now, as you can see, it's half empty.' The young archaeologist flicked a couple of her skinny plaits over her shoulder and pouted at the archive material spread out in front of her. 'Look, I really haven't got time for this. I was told you'd be able to help me with new information, but a lot of these articles and journals I've already seen.'

Trish wondered what Lincoln thought of her. He'd fancy her, probably, falling prey to her petite self-assurance – although she'd have to take better care of her skin or she'd look weatherbeaten in no time.

'I was only going through these boxes myself on Friday morning – one of your colleagues asked to look at what we'd got and it was certainly all here then.'

'Well, it obviously isn't now, is it?' Beth's fine eyebrows went up, her sunburnt forehead wrinkling.

'If you can wait, I'll give my assistant a ring, see if she

might've put some of it back in a different place.' Not that Briony ever misfiled anything…

'Don't bother.' And Beth Tarrant was gone.

Back at the dig, Beth felt ashamed of how rude she'd been to the woman at the library, but she'd been counting on finding out more about the 1956 dig. She needed to read more of what Roper-Reid had written about it, instead of concentrating on her grandfather's accounts. Over brunch yesterday, Troy had told her how he'd acquired some papers of Paul Roper-Reid's, and although they didn't relate directly to the Barbury dig, they did reveal a lot about the man himself.

'Did you know he was a skilled cartoonist?'

'Really?' She'd been surprised, and then remembered a little album she'd found when she was small, probably meant for autographs but full instead of pen-and-ink drawings of Grandpa Alf with his moustache and glasses; of her grandmother, Ailsa, in a polka-dot dress with a voluminous skirt. 'Yes,' she'd said, realizing. 'I did. Where did you find all this stuff of his?'

'Someone was selling it on eBay,' he said loftily as if he didn't want to give too much away.

But where was he now?

Josh dropped down beside her, ready for another day's work. He'd begged a mini digger off a builder friend to speed things up, and was keen to try it out. 'No Troy this morning? I was counting on the extra manpower.'

She put her hands on her hips. 'Why didn't you tell me you'd been through the archives at the library?'

'Me? What archives?'

'Don't look so innocent! All the material they've got on the earlier excavations. You were there Friday morning. The librarian told me.'

'I was here all day Friday – we both were, trying to make up for the time we lost with that stupid accident.'

'Then who –?' She stopped herself. It couldn't have been Troy. He'd come straight from Heathrow on Friday afternoon after flying in from the States. So, who else could it have been? 'Never mind. Listen, I found something on my grandfather's plans the other night. I think he'd detected another grave, next to Abbot William.'

Josh looked doubtful. 'There's not enough room.'

'He'd marked another area, possibly outside the chapel walls. I know nothing showed up on the survey, but once we knew we'd found the walls, we didn't survey outside again.'

'Beth, it's beyond our remit. We're excavating the crypt under the chapel, not odd graves outside it.'

'One grave, that's all.'

'But what do you expect to find? There's no time now, even if we could justify it.'

Now he was annoying her, acting the boss, denying her the opportunity…

No, she wouldn't fall out with him the way her grandfather had fallen out with Paul Roper-Reid. 'Let me go and fetch the plans and you can see for yourself.'

Ignoring his protests, she jogged back across Abbey Green to her flat. She bounded up the uneven stairs and into her room, flinging wide the wardrobe door and tugging the briefcase down from the shelf so she could get the plans.

Except the plans weren't there. The briefcase still held her notes and other papers, but Grandpa Alf's original plans were gone.

Her mind raced. Only Troy knew she'd got the plans and where she kept them. Only Troy had been into her bedroom...

She pulled her phone out and scrolled until she found his number. She suddenly realized he could've Skyped her from anywhere on Tuesday night. She'd assumed he was still in the States but...So it could've been Troy at the library on Friday morning who didn't put everything back.

What could Troy want with her grandfather's plans? What significance had he seen in them that she hadn't? And where the fuck was he?

She jogged more slowly back to the abbey, less excited now than apprehensive.

Josh looked as if he was braced for an argument.

'You're right.' She held her hands up, conciliatory. 'Let's concentrate on digging down to Abbot William and getting his tomb open. It's what we came here to do.'

She thought he'd want to know what changed her mind, but instead he clambered into the cab of the mini digger and turned the ignition key. He simply wanted to get on with it.

34

When Lincoln and Pam returned to the museum, Marjorie's dandelion clock of a head popped up over a display of Barbury Abbey mugs and tea towels.

'Have you come to see Melvyn? I'll give him a tinkle.'

While they waited, Pam asked her when she'd first noticed that exhibits were going missing.

'That was the funny thing. We weren't sure they *were* going missing at first. Things kept moving around. I'm sure Melvyn thought we were putting them back in the wrong place after we'd cleaned them. I know we're all getting on a bit, but we're not doolally yet!'

Pam brought out the evidence bag containing the broken piece of terracotta. 'Could this be one of the exhibits that went missing?'

'Oh, I know what that is! I backed my car into a planter outside the accommodation block a couple of weeks ago and smashed the edge off it. The bits have been lying around in the gutter ever since!'

'We found it in Greg Baverstock's room.'

Marjorie chuckled. 'He told me he was a bit of a beachcomber, always picking things up. How is he? I do hope he gets better soon. Such a nice man, although he was obviously having some sort of –'

But before she could tell them, Melvyn Potts beetled into the foyer, clipboard and pencil in hand.

In his office, they told him that although most of the stolen exhibits would eventually be returned, he may find that others had gone for good. Lincoln popped open a brown cardboard box containing a tubby pottery Venus in a nest of straw. 'You may want to check that the one in your display case is the genuine article and not a clever copy.'

The Facilities Manager's face registered dismay at the amount of work that lay ahead of him.

Marjorie caught them as they left. 'I worry that poor Mr Baverstock was having trouble with someone.'

'Oh?'

'He came in here all the time when he wasn't actually digging. On Monday, I think it was, I heard him on the phone to someone. It all got quite heated. I had to ask him to keep it down.'

'Could you tell what the call was about or who it was from?'

'I'd say it was personal, a gentleman's voice, someone he called Preston.'

Back at Barley Lane, an internet search brought up an unexpectedly long list of local people called Preston, with no obvious way of narrowing it down. Pam tried to call Rachel Fielder to see if she recognised the name as someone Greg had crossed swords with –

or whose wife he'd slept with – but she wasn't answering.

Lincoln collided with a stack of cardboard boxes. 'I thought Trading Standards were taking these?'

'Someone called,' said Breeze, waiting by the kettle. 'They'll collect them next week.'

'Not till then?' The phone went, the Guvnor asking about the paperwork for the CPS, what to do about the Gomez murder now the prime suspect was dead. Lincoln felt like telling him that's what a Chief Super got paid to deal with, but instead he told him it was in hand and he was more concerned right now with finding out who killed Sandy McFarlane.

'It's getting very messy, Jeff.'

'What, messier than McFarlane murdering his brother-in-law's brother-in-law?'

'What? Damn it, you're supposed to make my life easier, not complicate it.'

Lincoln put the phone down. 'What are we missing?' He stared at the whiteboard, hoping the answer would leap out at him. 'Or who?'

'Or whom,' said Pam. 'The girl who was in bed with Adrian Gomez – did we ever track her down?'

'Tia or Kia or Mia? No, we didn't.' He ran his hands through his hair. Where would you start looking for a girl whose name and description were a mystery? 'Gracie didn't seem to know her name, did she? Probably just a one-night stand.' Or in Adrian's case, a one-day stand.

Pam thought for a minute. 'Did anyone visit him in hospital, apart from us and Sandy? I'll go over to Presford General, see if Rachel's there and ask if anyone else came in to see Gomez.'

'Good idea. And look in on Baverstock while you're there, just in case there's been any change.'

35

Her name wasn't Kia or Mia or Tia, but Pia, as Pam found out when she dropped into the hospital to ask who'd visited Adrian Gomez. One of the nurses told her straightaway because she knew the girl, knew where she lived and where she worked.

'Pia Thompson,' she said. 'Works in Superdrug, or did. My daughter's probably got a number for her. They used to be mates a while back.'

By the time Pam got back to Barley Lane, the nurse had messaged her daughter, who'd messaged Pia to say the police were asking about her. Pia had decided to make the first move and had presented herself at the front desk a few minutes earlier.

Lincoln brought the young girl a Diet Coke from the machine, a coffee for himself and tea for Pam.

'Tell us what happened when Adrian got stabbed.'

Pia, twenty years old, skinny and pale, stroked the sides of the can as she told them. 'Me and Ade were, y'know, in bed and I heard something breaking in the hall. Ade jumps up and he's trying to get dressed and I'm putting my things back on, and she's making a noise like, y'know, like an animal, and she comes tearing into the bedroom, effing and blinding. And he tells me to get the fuck out, so I grab my phone, I grab his phone too 'cos it's got photos on what I sent him, photos I wouldn't want her or anybody else to see. I was gonna give him his phone back next time I saw him only when I went to the hospital he said, no, hang onto it for now, so I did.'

She placed two smartphones on the table, virtually identical. Passed one across. 'You probably want this, don't you?'

Pam took it, passed it to Lincoln. 'Did you see Gracie attack Adrian?'

Pia shook her head. 'I thought she was punching him, with her fists, like. Then I saw on my phone there was a man rushed to hospital with stab wounds, and people were tweeting which flats it was and so I knew.'

'Did you know he was stealing exhibits from the museum?'

She snorted with laughter, covering her mouth with a hand that had rings on every finger. 'From the museum? Is that where Lina got all that junk from?'

'You know Lina?'

'I don't *know* her, but I know she had all these boxes of rubbishy ornaments what she was trying to sell on eBay.' Another guffaw. 'No one was fucking interested, so she was stuck with them!'

Or Adrian was. Lincoln thought of the stacks of brown boxes in the little house off the London road. The stacks of brown boxes that were in the corridor here. 'You know where Lina is now?'

'Lina?' Pia made a face as if she hadn't a clue, but then she said, 'It'll be on his phone, won't it? She was messaging him all the time, like she didn't trust him to do anything without having her breathing down his neck every thirty seconds. But then again, they was very fond of each other, underneath all that. She's moving out to Spain permanent, like, but she's still got a flat in town, somewhere near the Half Moon Centre. It'll be on Ade's phone.'

Before Lincoln had even begun to think about going round to Lina's flat, Kylie, the woman with Gomez's spare key, texted Breeze. *"Lina round at Adrian's. Looks like she's spring-cleaning."*

'We should get round there,' Breeze said, 'before she destroys evidence we might need.'

When they got there, a silver Astra estate, parked on double yellow lines outside with its tailgate open, was steadily filling up with boxes and bags, padded envelopes and bubble wrap. Lina Cox was clearly moving her operation elsewhere.

Lincoln and Breeze went in through the open front door. Someone was banging about upstairs, shifting crates around, slamming drawers.

'What about the sister?' Woody had asked at the last briefing. 'Adrian's sister. Lina Cox. Could she have killed McFarlane? If she thought he'd killed Adrian?'

On the stairs, where she'd discarded them when she came in, were Lina's jacket, her handbag, a pair of shoes. Breeze picked them up, looked at the soles. Turned them so Lincoln could see they were white with chalk, the way Breeze's soles had been white after calling at McFarlane's bungalow.

'I think Woody was right,' said Lincoln. He started up the stairs.

36

Rachel drove back to Wayne Preston's house and waited. No sign of the lad on the motorbike today. Towards the end of the afternoon, a woman came out into the garden at the side of the house and took her washing in off the line. She hadn't long gone in when a black van with *Preston Tree Surgeon* on the side pulled up in the sloping yard at the front.

The door slid back, a man got out: Wayne Preston, fifties, six foot, sixteen stone, tanned, in khaki shorts and CAT work boots the colour of sand. He opened the back of the van, reached in, pulled out a chainsaw and a trough of tools.

Easily strong enough, tall enough, to punch Greg in the face and knock him down. And Rachel felt easily angry enough to drive her car into the back of his van while he was standing there, reaching in.

But she resisted the urge. What good would it do?

She got out of her car and walked steadily towards him. 'Mr Preston?'

He twisted round at the sound of her voice. 'That's right. Can I help you?'

Out of the corner of her eye, she saw the woman come out

onto the front porch, her hands clasped in front of her nervously as if she expected trouble.

'I've come about Greg Baverstock,' Rachel said. 'Can I come inside?'

37

Rosamund Tarrant hadn't stood on this spot for sixty years. How much the abbey towered over everything! How utterly insignificant it still made her feel!

The dig her father led here in 1956 looked so much like this one. How little the technology had moved on, the simple digging and scraping, robotic in its tedium (she always thought) but still needing the human touch, the human senses so vital to doing the task properly. And now, with rain on the horizon, they were having to put a tent up, an old-fashioned canvas tent that would make everything sticky and damp. There was no technology on earth that could stop the weather spoiling things.

She was thankful her daughter, Beth, had taken to archaeology in a way that she, herself, had not.

As a little girl of eight, Rosamund had been thrilled to be taken along on that dig, sure that her role was to keep her father company whenever Ailsa, her mother, was off doing something else on another part of the site, usually with someone else like Paul Roper-Reid.

Rosamund had been a little bit in love with Uncle Paul, as she called him. He was handsome in a way she knew, secretly, that her father was not. He and Auntie Liz brought their son Neville with them because he'd had measles and they didn't like to leave him with his grandparents.

Neville was nine and handsome too, except he wore glasses which spoiled it a bit, but he was clever and brave, and was always coming up with games they could play while the grown-ups were working or having a lie-down.

Uncle Paul was a terrific cartoonist, drawing pictures of everyone on the dig, including her and Neville. She wished now she'd kept more of those mementoes from that summer. She remembered especially a little flip book he'd made, a series of drawings showing Neville, little by little, falling out of a tree onto the grass below. If you flipped through the pages very fast, it looked like an animated cartoon: Neville falling from the tree and landing on the ground with a bump.

Her eighth birthday fell in the middle of the first week of the dig – what turned out, of course, to be the *only* week of the dig – and her mother had given her a Timex, her very first watch, with a bright red leather strap. Rosamund was so proud of it, she'd gone around showing everyone, all the students, Uncle Paul and Auntie Liz.

Neville pooh-poohed it. 'That's nothing!' he said. 'I got a bike for *my* birthday. It's got four gears and the lights run off a dynamo, and it's got a saddlebag…'

Rosamund had clamped her hands over her ears. She didn't want to hear.

They were going to organise a party for her on Abbey Green,

just some special treats on a trestle table, balloons and silly hats. She could blow out the candles on her cake.

And then Auntie Liz came over and said she couldn't find Neville and did Rosamund know where he'd got to?

'I haven't seen him since lunchtime. Perhaps he went into the abbey.' Even though they'd both been told not to stray out of sight of the grown-ups.

'I shouldn't think so,' said Auntie Liz, looking even more worried. 'And now I can't find your Uncle Paul.'

'Paul took Ailsa to pick up Ros's birthday cake,' her father said. 'Maybe he went with them.'

'I'll go and look for Neville in the abbey,' Rosamund had offered, feeling very heroic, volunteering. She hared off across Abbey Green, hoping the grown-ups were watching how fast she could run, even though she was only eight today.

She knew where Neville might have gone. The excavations and the abbey almost met at the west end of the building where there was a little porch you could hide in, with a stone staircase winding all the way up until it came out on a sort of platform where the bells were. It was an excellent place to hide if you didn't want to be found, and she'd bet anything that's where Neville was hiding.

As soon as Rosamund stepped into the porch, she knew she'd been right. She could hear sounds on the floor over her head, Neville playing soldiers or cowboys, thumping around in among the bell ropes like they'd done the other day, the two of them, him being the sheriff and her being the Indian he assumes is a brave until he discovers she's a squaw in disguise.

She clambered up the steps, twisting, turning, the sounds from the bell tower getting louder, not sounding like Neville at all, more like someone being hurt or –

Rosamund froze at the top of the stone steps, unable to make sense of what she saw. Mummy with her pretty dress all bunched up, standing against the wall with Uncle Paul leaning against her. She had her head on his shoulder, her lovely long hair hanging down.

Whatever they were doing, Rosamund knew it was terrible, something she shouldn't have seen. She started back down the steps, but her father had come up behind her, his eyes fixed on the very sight she didn't think he ought to see.

All she could remember then was the way he bundled her down the triangular stone steps, both of them stumbling and slipping until they reached the bottom.

'You mustn't tell anyone what you saw, Rosamund,' he'd said, gripping her wrist and pulling her across Abbey Green so fast, her feet hardly touched the grass. 'No one, not ever.'

She knew she'd done something unforgivable. She should never have gone looking for Neville. It was all his fault.

The paper cloth on the trestle table fluttered in the breeze, weighted down by plates of teacakes and buttered brown bread, jam and lemon curd that Auntie Liz had made herself, and bottles of cherry pop. There was Neville, already tucking in.

'Where were you?' Rosamund asked to give herself something else to think about.

'The students were showing me something,' he said mysteriously. 'They're going to play a joke on Rodney, that one who's always making out he knows everything. I can't tell you because they've sworn me to secrecy.'

He made himself sound so important but she didn't care. She tried to eat something but it was like trying to eat a paper napkin. All she could think of was her mother's hair hanging down on Uncle Paul's shoulder. The look on her father's face.

'I feel sick,' she said, and plodded away to the far side of the excavations. It wouldn't show if she was sick where they'd been digging. It would all blend in.

A couple of the students were still digging. Weren't they stopping now it was starting to look like rain? She stood watching them for a moment or two, hating her mother, hating Uncle Paul, hating Neville for making her go to the abbey to look for him.

The students laid their spades on the ground by the hole they'd dug and walked away. Rosamund snatched the watch off her wrist, the Timex she was so proud of, and tossed it into the hole. She didn't care if she never saw it again. How could her mother give her a birthday present like that and then do whatever it was that upset her father so much?

'I don't want your stupid present!' She stared down at the watch, wanting to cry. She could still get the watch back if she was quick.

But then the students came back across Abbey Green, laughing, up to something as Neville had said. Auntie Liz was calling her, calling for the birthday girl to come and blow out the candles on her cake.

Across Abbey Green, just as it was getting dark, Rosamund watched the candles gutter in the chilly air, illuminating the faces of her mother and Auntie Liz, Uncle Paul and Neville. Her father was nowhere to be seen.

She'd looked round for him, suddenly terrified something awful had happened, more awful than whatever had happened in the bell tower. And there he was, standing on the edge of the excavations, looking down, looking so alone she'd wanted to wrap him up and take him home, just the two of them, where they'd be safe for ever and ever.

Sixty years. Where had the time gone? Rosamund Tarrant hitched her rucksack higher on her shoulders and pulled her rain hat down. First of all, she'd slip into the abbey to say a little prayer. Then she'd go and look for Beth.

38

'Got it!' Pam sat back from her computer, exultant. 'Preston's a tree surgeon. Look at his logo!' She pointed to her screen and then at the CCTV image of the black van outside the museum.

Woody looked. 'Reckon that's what's on that sticker. Well done!'

'That van was outside the museum a couple of nights before Greg was beaten up. We thought it was waiting there for Gomez, but I bet you Preston was watching for a chance to confront Greg.'

She leapt up, grabbing her coat and bag.

Woody stood up too. 'Now hang on, Pam, you can't go over there on your own. If you're right about Preston being the man who attacked Baverstock, we know he's violent.'

She dropped her coat and bag back on the chair. 'I can't just sit here.'

'Give the boss a ring. Let him decide what to do next.' Woody sat down again. 'Any luck getting hold of Rachel Fielder?'

'No. She wasn't at the hospital. They haven't seen her all day.' Pam remembered Rachel's parting remark, that she'd know the name of Greg's married woman when she saw it. Supposing she'd found his list of contacts after all and had decided to take matters into her own hands? 'Better phone the boss,' she said, 'and let's hope Rachel doesn't go round there and do something stupid.'

39

At last, the gravestones in the floor of the crypt lay uncovered. Beth looked round for Troy, wishing he was here to witness this important moment, but he was nowhere to be seen and he wasn't answering his phone. When he did turn up, she'd give him a piece of her mind.

'They all seem so modest,' Josh said as he took photos of each of the stone slabs as they emerged – six in all. 'Their names, the date they died, nothing else.'

The inscriptions had been remarkably well preserved beneath their protective layers of soil. To think that nearly a millennium had passed since human feet had trodden on these flagstones!

Most of the graves had sunk into the floor, but one alone stood proud: the last resting place of Abbot William Spere. The next challenge would be to lift the lid of the tomb and examine what lay inside.

Josh was right: there really was no space for another grave between the Abbot's and the wall. If her grandfather's plan was accurate, and he'd found evidence of a grave *outside* the wall, excavating it would be impossible without going through the whole rigmarole of getting permission, resurveying, taking samples…

Maybe another year.

'Oh shit, it's starting to rain.' He held his hand out and glowered up at the sky. 'We should've got a tent up before we got this much uncovered.'

The next half hour was taken up with the whole team struggling to set up a marquee to protect the sunken part of the dig. Rain clouds gathered bulk on the horizon, the light turned silvery, the air tasted metallic.

Josh made a show of looking round him. 'So, what's happened to Wonder Boy?' With the tent over them, they were clearing away the last of the rubble from around Abbot William's tomb. 'He should be here for this. Haven't fallen out, have you?'

On cue, Troy appeared above them, his laptop bag slung across his body. Behind him, the sky was darkening. He called down to them. 'So, you're not going to look for that other grave?'

'What other grave, Troy?' She peered up at him. He had the cheek to be clutching the plans he'd stolen from her flat! 'There is no other grave!'

'Not down there but it must be here, outside the walls! And I'm going to prove it to you!' And he chucked his bag down on the grass and vanished from view.

'Oh, for fuck's sake!' Beth threw down her tools and went after him.

Lightning slashed the sky. Seconds later, thunder rumbled across. God moving the furniture, as her mother always said.

The next thing Beth heard was the rasp of an engine, the chug of a mini digger starting up. As she drew level with the top of the trench, she saw Troy wrestling with the gears of the digger and lurching across Abbey Green.

'What the fuck's he playing at?' Josh was behind her, vaulting out of the trench and running across the grass in pursuit. The digger was going round in circles at first, but then Troy mastered the steering and headed straight for his target.

The mystery grave, Beth guessed.

'Did you put him up to this?' Josh seized her by the arm as they watched Troy trying to manoeuvre. The bucket of the digger went down, swiping at the grass. Troy grabbed at the controls as if he wasn't sure which joystick did what.

'Of course I didn't! He's convinced there's another grave next to Abbot William's. I think he thinks it's St Aedina's.'

Josh swung her round. 'Aedina's nowhere near here! They've proved that, finding her seal! She was carried off to bloody Pembrokeshire!'

Beth nodded towards Troy. 'Try telling him that.'

Another shock of lightning. God moved some more furniture. Big raindrops began to fall.

The bucket bit into the ground and peeled off a layer of turf. Troy's face was radiant. He was going to get at that grave, come hell or high water.

The tracks of the digger crept near the edge of the trench. Too near. As the next shaft of lightning came running down the sky, Troy and the digger tipped up and fell into the crypt.

40

Anna Preston couldn't seem to look Rachel in the face. They sat across from each other at a table in the Prestons' conservatory, warm by this time of the day, although the sky was filling with dirty grey rain clouds.

'How long were you seeing him for?' Rachel asked, wondering what Greg had seen in this dumpy woman who must be at least as old as him, maybe older.

'After that first time in December, two or three times, maybe four.'

'I can't believe you can sit there so calmly and tell me that.'

At last Anna looked up. 'Rachel, it isn't what you think.'

'Oh, it never bloody is, is it!'

'Greg and I talked, that's all we did. And just lately, we've kept in touch by text. Nothing more.'

Rachel's eyes took in the smart rattan furniture, the floor lamps, the grey-brown rug like a load of voles sewn together. From here she could see the Prestons' paddock rolling away from the house down towards the river she'd driven over earlier. The rooks in the trees at the bottom of the paddock were making the sort of racket that would drive her mad if she lived here.

'Tell me, then, what did you talk about?'

Anna folded her hands on the table. 'Wayne and I lost our youngest son last year. He was fourteen. Chas. He died playing rugby at school.'

For the first time, Rachel noticed the family photos on the side table, a few years old: Wayne and Anna, the two boys she'd seen messing around with the motorbike, and a younger boy. The dead one. She felt giddy. 'I'm sorry, I –'

'Chas was in Greg's class at one time so he knew us, asked if we wanted to talk it through. Wayne…' She glanced across to the workshop where her husband was sawing a tree branch. 'Wayne just gets on with things. I'm different. I needed someone to talk to. And so did Greg.'

'But I –'

Anna lifted her hand to shush her. 'Greg didn't find it easy to talk, not even to me, but he was so good, sharing some of the ways he's found to cope since he lost Rory. Sometimes you just need to be able to talk about someone you've lost. You don't need anyone to sympathise, you just need them to let you talk, to let you remember.'

Rachel sat quietly, angry with herself for jumping to conclusions, for not being someone Greg could talk to, for letting him down. Then she recalled the reason for her visit. 'It was Wayne who attacked him, wasn't it?'

'I'm sorry, Rachel, really I am. He saw I'd got a text from Greg the other day and got it into his head we were having an affair. Last week, he was doing a job near the abbey and recognised

Greg. He watched to see where he was staying and then waited to have it out with him. Rachel, believe me, he never meant to put him in hospital like that. Wayne says Greg lashed out at him when he surprised him on the landing and they got into a punch-up. There was a bit of pushing and shoving, Greg fell on the floor and didn't get up.'

'Your stupid husband smashed his room up.'

'He was angry. He didn't know what he was doing. When he realized he'd knocked Greg out, he panicked and ran.' Anna got up and went into the kitchen, coming back with an iPhone. 'He picked this up without thinking.'

Rachel took hold of Greg's phone, wrapping her fingers round it as if she never wanted to let it go. 'You know he may not wake up again, don't you?'

'If we could take any of it back…' Anna opened her hands imploringly. 'Is there a chance Rory's skull weakness is genetic? That Greg's got it too? It's not as if Wayne hit him that hard…'

Rachel jerked her head towards stupid Wayne and his workshop. He was chopping logs like a backwoodsman. 'Is he going to turn himself in to the police? Because if he doesn't, I will.' She stood up. 'And I'm sorry about your son.'

As she walked back to her car, it was all she could do not to charge at Wayne Preston, seize the axe from his hands and set about him with it. The stupid, stupid man.

Instead, as she strode past his black van, she leaned in through the open door and let the handbrake off. She didn't wait to see how long it took to roll down the paddock and into the stream.

41

Troy wasn't badly hurt, even though Josh threatened to slaughter him for wrecking the digger. An ambulance was called anyway and people came out of the abbey and the museum to see if they could help.

Rain drummed on the roof of the tent as a paramedic checked Troy over and pronounced him fit. 'Might hit you later, though,' the young girl warned. 'Delayed reaction. Make sure you've got someone with you tonight, just in case.'

'That certainly won't be me!' Beth glared down at him. 'You deserved to break your fucking neck!'

'Lillibet, that's no way to talk!'

Beth looked up to see Josh helping her mother climb gingerly down into the crypt. 'Mum! What are you doing here? I didn't tell you I was coming here!'

'No, but I saw it on your webpage.' She smiled slyly.

An elderly white-haired lady from the museum had brought a tray of tea across in the rain so, although it was a bit diluted, it was very welcome.

'I remember the earlier dig,' she confided proudly. 'They let you get right up close to where they were digging.'

'What in God's name made you think St Aedina was buried here?' Josh asked Troy.

'I bought some stuff on the internet,' he said. He reached for his bag and pulled out a sheaf of papers.

Beth noticed her mother's eyes narrowing at the sight of them.

'Your grandfather's plans, Beth – that fuzzy part on the edge confirmed what I'd already worked out from this.' He held out to her a small sketchbook, open at a drawing of a pretty woman in a polka-dot dress, Fifties-style, tumbling through space onto what was obviously a gravestone. Above her, a man was peering down in consternation. A flowing script captioned the drawing: *And they, before their lust was curbed, a saintly grave disturbed.*

'Don't you see, that's Aedina's grave! With her wyvern emblem on it, just like the seal! That's Roper-Reid and some woman, falling through the floor of the crypt and discovering her grave!'

'No,' said Beth's mother, stepping forward. 'That's Uncle Paul and my mother falling out of the bell loft in the abbey.'

42

'I feel kind of stupid.' They stood in the abbey porch, gazing down at a memorial stone, worn almost smooth by the passage of thousands of pairs of feet over the centuries: St Aedina's wyvern, almost impossible to make out unless you knew what you were looking for.

'Was your mother killed?' Josh asked Rosamund, holding up the drawing of Beth's grandmother falling out of the bell loft in a froth of petticoats.

'Not then,' said Rosamund, snatching the sketchbook from him. 'Later, coming off her motorbike.'

'So, then, this drawing…?'

'Artistic licence. They came down the steps from the bell loft and Uncle Paul – Paul – spotted the emblem because of the way the light was falling on it.'

'So Aedina's been here all the time, hidden in plain sight.' Beth felt quite deflated after all that. The "ballast" her mother had "jettisoned" must have included this sketchbook, probably given to Ailsa by Roper-Reid himself. Not so much jettisoned as flogged on eBay, where Troy had found them!

'So, the seal of Aedina that turned up in Wales?' Josh scratched his head.

'Distraction,' Troy said wearily. 'Probably taken there to fool the men pursuing her to the grave.' He put his head in his hands. 'Things haven't been going so well in the States. I lost tenure, came home early. I needed something groundbreaking to put me back up the ladder. When I saw that smudgy bit on your grandfather's plans, I guess I convinced myself it was the grave that was shown in that cartoon.'

'More likely it was just a smudge,' Beth's mother said kindly. 'Resting his hand on the paper before the ink was dry.'

Beth patted him on the shoulder. 'We still haven't opened the tomb of the Angling Abbot. Who knows what we're going to find inside?'

'Some dried-out old bones and some fishing flies, knowing my luck!'

'Come on,' said Josh. 'Who knows, we might find the Holy Grail.'

'And Aedina?' Beth's mother stood looking down at the worn lettering.

'Let's leave her,' said Beth, drawing her away. 'For now.'

43

'Didn't I tell you I'd find somebody?' Trish pushed a tall, stooping man into the kitchen where Lincoln was having coffee. It had been a tough day. As well as sorting out the paperwork for the CPS so Gracie Bell got a fair hearing, he'd seen Wayne Preston released on bail for the attack on Greg Baverstock. He wasn't in the mood for visitors.

'The name's Johnnie Bird,' the elderly man said. 'I know Trish's dad through the U3A, the University of the Third Age.'

Lincoln was at a loss until Trish reminded him. 'I wondered if anyone had any snapshots of the 1956 dig, remember?'

Lincoln sat back, feeling ambushed. Trish had said it as a joke. He hadn't seriously imagined…

'I was one of the student volunteers,' Johnnie went on. 'My first dig. Very exciting. We got up to some mischief!'

He lowered himself stiffly onto a kitchen chair and laid a small snapshot album out on the table. Together, they turned the pages, Johnnie commenting on the people in the photos. Alfred Lever was a bit of a cold fish. Paul Roper-Reid was rather dashing. Mrs Lever was quite a stunner. Mrs Roper-Reid was a bit of a worrier.

'Trish was asking about a skeleton,' Johnnie said. 'Confession time!'

And he explained how half a dozen of them had decided to play a trick on a rather bumptious student called Rodney. 'Thought he knew everything, you know the sort! Under cover of darkness, we beavered away digging this grave. Made it look really authentic until we realized we'd dug it the wrong way, but no matter.' He winked and carried on. 'A couple of us were medical students, got hold of a teaching skeleton. We were only going to borrow it, weren't we, clean it up afterwards and put it back! Everything was set for Rodney to be the first one to find this bloody grave and tell us all about his astounding discovery!'

He flipped to a photograph of a dull grey day, rain falling, everything being dismantled. 'But, of course, they struck camp early, as it were, on account of the weather and some sort of disagreement among the boffins. And our poor old skeleton had to stay there!' He grinned, a man in his eighties, thrilled to relive that heady summer at the abbey. 'Fancy it turning up now! I shall have to get in touch with these archaeologists and own up!'

Lincoln guessed the old boy would rather enjoy that.

Much later, on the back steps with Trish, he shut his eyes and listened to the sound of the traffic, the distant whine of a mainline train speeding through the night, the shriek of blackbirds chasing through the undergrowth.

'The Guvnor's retiring this year, not next,' he told her. 'Barley Lane could be closed by the end of the year.'

'What'll that mean for you? Working out of Park Street instead?'

Could he face that, having Presford as a base instead of Barbury?

'Or I could finish, find something else to do.'

'Like what? A job in security?' She elbowed him in the ribs.

'I can think of worse things.' He'd heard that morning that Greg Baverstock had regained consciousness, would probably make a full recovery, but it'd been a close-run thing. How your life can change in the space of a minute!

She picked up her coffee mug, clashed it gently against his. 'One day at a time,' she said with a grin. 'One day at a time.'

Also By Nikki Copleston

The Shame of Innocence

Stage-struck teenager Emma Sherman is found dead on a Wiltshire golf course – no witnesses, no suspects. Detective Inspector Jeff Lincoln gets little help from Emma's neurotic mother, but he's sure she knows something. When explicit photos of Emma are found hidden in an abandoned summer house, Lincoln's sure they hold clues to her murder. But who was the photographer, and why doesn't Lincoln's boss want him to find out?

Days later another teenage girl is brutally murdered and her body is dumped in a country lane. The disappearance of a third teenage girl makes Lincoln realise he's facing a more dangerous enemy than he first imagined.